TAKE A BITE

The Rhys Davies
Short Story Award Anthology

Julia Bell is a writer and Reader in Creative Writing at Birkbeck where she is the Course Director of the MA in Creative Writing. Her work includes poetry, essays and short stories published in the *Paris Review*, *Times Literary Supplement*, *The White Review*, *Mal Journal*, *Comma Press*, and recorded for the BBC. Her most recent book-length essay *Radical Attention* has just been published by Peninsula Press. Twitter: @JuliaBell

Elaine Canning is an Irish writer living in Swansea and has many years' experience working as a public engagement professional in arts and culture. She is currently Head of Cultural Engagement at Swansea University and Executive Officer of the Dylan Thomas Prize. She has an MA and PhD in Hispanic Studies from Queen's University, Belfast and an MA in Creative Writing from Swansea University. As well as having written a monograph and papers on Spanish Golden-Age drama, she has also published several short stories. Her debut novel, *The Sandstone City*, is forthcoming with Aderyn Press in 2022.

TAKE A BITE

The Rhys Davies
Short Story Award Anthology

Edited by Elaine Canning
Selected and Introduced by Julia Bell

PARTHIAN

Parthian, Cardigan SA43 1ED
www.parthianbooks.com
ISBN 978-1-913640-63-7
First published in 2021 © the contributors
Edited by Carly Holmes
Cover design by Syncopated Pandemonium
Typeset by Elaine Sharples www.typesetter.org.uk
Printed by 4edge Limited

Contents

Introduction

Julia Bell

Rhys Davies, whose legacy is this prize, was a prodigious and prolific writer. He made his living by the pen, producing over his lifetime some twenty novels and over one hundred short stories. Exiled from Wales in part because of his sexuality, he nonetheless continued to live there in his mind; the voices and stories of the Welsh – especially those who came from the valleys where he grew up, and especially women – call out loudly in his pages, to give us characters which are powerful and recognisable. There is a sense of touching history when we read him: these people, our ancestors, are brought vividly to life, and anyone with an interest in what lives were like for the women of the valleys would do well to read his work. But he is more than just an historical curio, he was also an extremely accomplished proponent of the form. Each piece gives us what a good short story must – an experience – namely it moves us, gives us a sense in a few short paragraphs that we might know these characters and care about them and about their concerns. His ear for speech is especially attuned, and at times when reading him I can almost hear the voices, crowded around the streets and pubs of the Rhondda, speaking to me as if they were in my own living room. His work is visceral and moving and deserves to be much better known. Anyone with an interest could start with the Parthian/Library of Wales edition of the short stories which contains many of his classics.

It was this sense of the experience that I was looking for when judging this competition – for twelve pieces which take us inside a character and which create a world for the reader. To quote Raymond Carver, 'if we're lucky, writer and reader alike, we'll finish the last line or two of a short story and then just sit for a minute, quietly. Ideally, we'll ponder what we've just written or read; maybe our hearts or intellects will have been moved off the peg just a little from where they were before. Our body temperature will have gone up, or down, by a degree.' This was my criteria: I wanted work which had the capacity to alter the body temperature, which was alive with character, voice and language.

There are many contemporary concerns riven throughout the pieces I selected and perhaps unsurprisingly, given that this is 2021, one of the overall themes to this selection is that of loss. Both Elizabeth Pratt in 'James, in During' and Giancarlo Gemin in 'Cure Time', reflect directly on aspects of the pandemic and the lockdown we have just experienced. Both of these pieces recreate the sense of claustrophobia and time dislocation which the long weeks of lockdown engendered, and the descriptions of grief, frustration and loneliness will resonate with many.

Other stories deal with family dynamics, and the consequences of loss – especially the pain of parenting children in these circumstances. The father and son relationship in Craig Hawes' 'Coat of Arms' is especially tender, as are the amusing descriptions of a day at a medieval re-enactment. In Chloë Heuch's 'Y Castell' we have the familiar Welsh holiday experience of a trip to the castle, except here the mother and her sons are still trying to come to terms with a recent divorce. In 'A Cloud of Starlings' by Philippa Holloway a mother tries to comfort her daughter

2

who is distressed by the dead birds which keep falling from the sky, while at the same time managing her grief for the daughter she wishes she'd had. In 'Conditions for an Avalanche' by Kate Lockwood Jefford, we get a visceral glimpse of life on the breadline, while grief burns up the characters and everything they touch.

The way we see each other is also a theme shared by several of the pieces. In 'Bird' by Jupiter Jones a strange encounter in the countryside is described with great tenderness from two different points of view, and in 'Juice' by Rosie Manning the rugby-playing Owen is revealed by his neighbour to be hiding some interesting secrets. In Susmita Bhattacharya's 'The Truth is a Dangerous Landscape' daughters reveal family secrets to their mother and await her response. The form is exactly right for these kinds of stories: glimpses of characters, small moments of dramatic irony, a touching moment of realisation. This is what the short form can do so well.

There are several pieces which thrilled me with their use of language too – the way the sentences flowed across the page with a flourish which moved beyond realism. The night at the pub in 'Half Moon, New Year' by Joshua Jones reads with the boozy tilt of a night on the lash, the chorus of voices and casual violence recreating both the chaos and vulnerability of getting blind drunk. In Brennig Davies' 'Dogs in a Storm', a woman is on the verge of a transformation and the sentences fizz with her frustration and nascent becoming.

Finally, Naomi Paulus' story 'Take a Bite', which begins the selection, is perhaps the closest to Rhys Davies' style in mixing both realism with a stylish linguistic flourish and an especially acute ear for dialogue. We follow Rhian back to her grandmother's house for a funeral with her mother and her aunts. There is a distance between Rhian and her family which is generational and feminist; Rhian is looking in from elsewhere at a life she grew up with, and the voices of the women are vivid and poetic. Here is a writer who listens to the world.

Each one of these stories creates a small moment that hopefully gives pause for something – what? – not thought, not initially anyway, but *feeling*. All good writing should be an experience for the reader, and to do that the good writer needs to be artful, deploying language and character in the service of creating that experience. The thought, the analysis, the essays, they come later, but the first question has to be: 'Does it move me?' and then, 'Am I convinced?' In the case of these twelve pieces the answer is most certainly, yes.

Take a Bite

Naomi Paulus

Esyllt arrived first.

She was the eldest of Rhian's mother's four sisters and it always mystified Rhian how a woman could have such a massive bust but be so completely not sexual. Just a kind of amorphous, fleshy protrusion from the front of her torso, like a benign cyst. Esyllt arrived through the back door, tits first, without introduction and seamlessly re-entered the conversation she had left on half the day before. The sisters didn't bother with greetings, or other meaningless pleasantries, because they were in permanent celestial orbit around each other, never apart for long enough.

Rhian wasn't sure whether Esyllt arrived with a tea towel in hand because she seemed to be already drying up as she crossed the threshold. A cog trained from birth to fit seamlessly into the mundane domestic machine. Rhian's mum, Gwen, turned from the sink and handed her oldest sister a pot like Esyllt was always standing waiting for it and she replied like the conversation was never paused.

'Well, finally, here we are.'

'The others are on their way.'

'Here we are.'

'They're on their way.'

There followed an unusual pause in conversation. If silence settled amongst the suds in that house, it never lasted long. Rhian watched the fairy motes swirl in the light from the kitchen window as they floated towards the black slate floor. Picking at the fraying end of the tea towel in her hands, she traced the light back to its source above the sink, where neat piles of dead flies were turning to dust on the windowsill. How apt, thought Rhian; dust to dust.

Her aunt had usurped her in the dishwashing receiving line, which downgraded Rhian from dryer to put-away-er. Eventually, she was handed the scrubbed and dried pot, giving her something else to do with her hands. It was the third Saturday morning in March and Rhian's aunts were gathering for an important event. Rhian had come home to join the ritual. Her grandmother, the mother of all, was still upstairs but she wouldn't be for much longer.

Once the pot was put away, Esyllt turned her attention to Rhian who was caught standing still again.

'How is life in the city, you?'

'Yes, good, thank you.'

'You're looking well. Is that a new haircut?'

Rhian nodded. There wasn't much else she could say. She felt guilty for leaving, for trying to carve out a space for herself in a place full of strangers. It was terrifying but it promised the possibility of becoming someone entirely new. She reached up her hand to smooth down her fringe. She knew that 'well' meant 'fat' and that it was a compliment, but the haircut had cost too much, and it felt like she was wearing a Mercedes symbol on her forehead.

Gwen hadn't noticed the new hairstyle yet but she didn't turn away from the sink to look. It had been dark the night before, when she'd gone to get Rhian from the train station, and she'd been understandably preoccupied that morning. It was an unusual sight to see Gwen washing up because she usually refused while Rhian's dad hunched his slipped discs over the bowl. The refusal was her one outlet of protest. She would not worship at the altar of domesticity; when it came to housewifery she would do everything but the kitchen sink. But that day was different.

The back door opened again and the two middle sisters, Helen and Wendy, came in chatting and let the cat in with them. They were both carrying deep pudding bowls wrapped in cling film and Rhian wondered how they had fitted through the narrow doorframe seemingly still side-by-side. Irish twins they were – well, Welsh twins. Born nine months apart within the same school year and, even though they were sixty, it still mattered. They took off their tall, dark hats and placed them on the kitchen table. Then they got to work.

'Where's Mam?'

'How are you, Es?'

'Any cake here?'

'Upstairs. Bathed, dressed and ready.'

'Bara brith in the tin.'

'I'm putting my trifle in the fridge.'

'Dew, dew the bus was slow.'

'Strawberries fresh from the market in it, mind.'

'It was going to happen one day.'

'That'll be nice.'

'I still can't believe it.'

'Where's Alys?'

With four of the five sisters in the same room, the conversation got harder to follow. Rhian pondered the mathematical conundrum: if there were four of her aunties in a room, how many different conversations could be had at once? Well, there was Mum and Esyllt, Mum and Helen, Mum and Wendy; then there was Esyllt and Helen, Esyllt and Wendy, and finally Helen and Wendy. So that was six in total, not including Rhian. However, there was no reason to assume that Esyllt was having the same conversation with Helen that Helen thought she was having with Esyllt. The relationship between the conversations was not necessarily reciprocal and that brought the total number possible to twelve. Although deafening, Rhian found the noise soothing. It rested just above the flapping tea towels, filling the air like a fine Welsh mist, drenching everything and drowning out her own thoughts.

Occasionally, one voice would shrill above the rest, amplified further when it bounced off the thick, stone walls of their cottage. It was the reason Rhian's father had slipped out earlier and was sitting outside in the cold. He had previously suggested that the women in the family he married into were descended from banshees, Cyhyraeth, because of the pitches they could reach. Comparing middle-aged women to decrepit, wailing harbingers was not particularly imaginative.

'You know I'm not good at all that. I'll come back in when they've settled,' was what he told Rhian. It is women's work, was what he meant. Women marked life's rituals, its comings and goings, with ceremony and compassion. Rhian's family was certainly not short on women. Her grandmother upstairs, Nana, was the oldest of fourteen girls. Rhian came from old breeding stock who had learnt the hard way that breastfeeding was not a natural contraceptive. She sometimes thought it was strange that all the sisters only had daughters. There were rumours in the village, usually sparked by the birth of yet another baby girl. Like Welsh Russian dolls popping out of each other in a long, long line stretching back to the beginning. A womb, within a womb, within a womb. Rhian didn't like to think about it, she had run away to try to break the chain.

'Seriously though, where is Alys?'

'Rhian, grab the broom, will you?'

'On her way apparently.'

'Helen's already spilt the sugar.'

'She lives next door, mun!'

'I've cleaned the table, ready for mixing.'

'Make sure you've hidden the curry powder.'

'The butter is already out to soften on the counter here.'

'Bloody hell, yes, we don't want a repeat of Wendy's last "coffee" cake.'

'Is the oven on ready?'

'Blew my bloody head off that cake did.'

Rhian did as she was told and mostly stayed out of the conversation, although she kept hold of every entangled thread because very occasionally interesting gossip was revealed.

She wondered when her grandmother would finally be able to come downstairs and what would happen when she did. She was still the matriarch after all and it was her party they were getting ready for. Last night, Rhian had painted Nana's nails while Gwen bathed her. Rhian chose Nana's favourite colour, Revlon Cadillac red, for her long thick claws which were all knuckles and gold rings like a hardened Mafia wife's. If Rhian's Nana had had the will to throw a punch – god knows she had the temper – she could have done some serious damage to a jawline. While the talons were drying, Rhian brushed out Nana's hair and curled it into a neat bun on the top of her head. Her chosen outfit was a deep purple suit from David Evans department store. It was well worn and well loved.

There would be many mouths to feed later and so there were many cakes to be baked. Welsh cakes, more bara brith, a Victoria sponge, scones and apple tarts. All of Nana's favourites had been specially requested. The bowl of shining apples, buffed to a sparkling crimson, was particularly appealing to Rhian. But they would soon be chopped and cooked until the fibres were denatured, the skins crisp and burnt, and the insides turned to mush.

The smell of charred flesh started to overpower the sweetness in the air as Esyllt's fingers melded to the oven and the first shriek rang out.

'Ow! I've burnt my bloody hand.'

'Rhian, grab more flour and sugar from the pantry, will you?'

'The oven is on then.'

'Welsh cakes need mixed spice too, Gwen.'

'Run it under the cold water.'

'Hocus, they just need cinnamon.'

'Do you have a sieve? I've lost a nail in the flour.'

'It's a family recipe.'

'Helen stop fussing, you're doing my head in.'

'There's cheek! I am the bloody family.'

'Have you called Alys? She should be here.'

Alys was the youngest sister. She had been babied, as youngest children are, and the other sisters blamed that for her maladjustment. Her name was followed in conversation by the phrase 'bless her' and a sad smile. Single and childless, she was a failed woman in her mother's eyes, infantilised forever. Rhian had inherited this feeling of pity but she had always been closest to Alys. The aunt who lived next door and always brought back holiday trinkets for the display shelf. Slowly the feeling was growing into a sense of admiration for a woman daring to live a different type of life. Alys had a secret and she had only told Rhian. It was so small and yet so radical that it gave Rhian hope.

'Someone put the kettle on, I need a brew.'

'Gladys up the road was stuck in the bath for three days last week.'

'I'll have one if you're making a pot.'

'Three full days, mind.'

'Is there another baking tray about?'

'I just thank god she was at the tap end.'

'Tea for me too, please.'

'You know, so she could drink from the tap like.'

'Bloody hell, there's times I can't be bothered to get out of the bath.'

'Pass us that rolling pin by there.'

'It's not funny, Esyllt, that's what kept her alive.'

'Rhian go check on your father, will you?'

'The tap end? Iesu Mawr.'

The excuse to leave was a welcome release for Rhian who loved her family but, well… but. She let herself out the back door with the cat twisting through her feet. The familiar feel of its fur against her shins was a small comfort. Outside, the morning shadows were long and low on the crispy grass. It was going to be a brilliantly sunny spring day, Rhian observed, as her socks stuck to the frost on the path.

Her father was sitting on a stool in the front garden, weekend broadsheet in his left elbow, cigarette in his right hand. He looked like a doorman and Rhian realised that from this position he would have welcomed each and every aunt on her arrival. Maybe this wasn't such a cop out after all; he was out here taking the edge off, softening their approach.

'Mam wants to know if you want some tea.'

'Yes please. That would be lovely. How's it going in there?'

'Okay. There's a lot of shouting. They're baking.'

'Lots to prepare for later. Best I stay out the way.'

As he puffed on the cigarette to catch his breath, Rhian

11

could hear every single word coming from the house. It was difficult to keep secrets on that street. She paused, next to the man who never felt the need to say anything at all, and enjoyed the relative quiet until her toes went numb. The heat of the sun was on her cheeks, so bright that when she closed her eyes she could still see the light. It felt good to be back somewhere on the slope downwards between the low mountains and deep valleys, even though she was back for a bad reason.

When Rhian reopened her eyes and readjusted to the brightness, the last of her aunts was waiting at the front gate, arranging her courage to enter. Alys was quieter than her older sisters; having to hide something can do that to you. It makes you afraid to talk for fear of giving yourself out. Stood still at the bottom of the garden, elbow deep in a family packet of crisps, she nodded a hello at Rhian. For a brief moment the sound of Alys crunching on roast chicken flavouring overpowered everything else, even the birds. Then came a clatter of falling pans and the second shriek. It was so loud and so piercing that even though Rhian knew it had come from inside the cottage, it felt like it came from someone standing right behind her.

Alys and Rhian's father were unfazed by the sound, they had been around the sisters too long, but the deafening call reminded Rhian why she was there. She wriggled her toes to bring them back to life and led her youngest aunt into the house. The act of accompanying was partly for Alys and partly for Rhian herself. She always felt stronger in a pair.

Rhian and Alys were put to work as soon as they opened the back door. Esyllt was growling orders from in front of the sink. Gwen was on her hands and knees picking up the contents of the pan cupboard that had fallen. Helen and

12

Wendy were kneading and rolling out the Welsh cake mix while correcting each other's techniques.

'No, not like that, Wend, let me do it.'

'Sally Morgan is coming over later, I saw her this morning—'

'Kettle's boiled.'

'—when I was on my way to speak to the priest.'

'Where is the sugar kept, Gwen?'

'I heard her husband was in trouble again.'

'Who wanted tea?'

'In trouble from shagging around, is he?'

'Everyone for tea it was.'

'Alys, make yourself useful please.'

Alys was instructed to join her middle sisters and stack up the fat, flat circles, ready for the griddle. On hearing this, the look Helen and Wendy exchanged made Rhian grit her back teeth together. She glared at them from her dusty mixing station at the other end of the kitchen table and tightened her fist around the wooden spoon. Rhian was combining ingredients – butter, sugar, flour – into the biggest bowls her mother could find. She felt each strained turn of the spoon around the circumference of the sludge like a crank forward in time, lurching them closer towards the countdown. With every turn of her hand, the temperature in the kitchen increased. Sweat was starting to form on the menopausal jowls that hung off the faces of her aunts, running down their flapping necks and crevices, to the sagging nipples that ruptured from their bulging, waxy skin. Rhian kept churning the mix, thickening it up for the oven.

'I've been so busy the last few days. I haven't had time to swing a cat.'

'Poor sod she is, that one.'

'It's room, you idiot, room to swing a cat.'

'Who?'

'We're lucky I'm on the parish council to have got the hall at such short notice.'

'Sally Morgan, mun!'

'Ooh, la-de-da, Esyllt. We'd have found somewhere else if we needed.'

'I think it's disgusting, treating your wife like that.'

Rhian whipped the eggs into the flour in such frenzy that white splatter covered the front of her black suit. It was difficult to stay calm when the activity level around her was not so much a flurry as an avalanche. The sisters, although each had different personalities and preferences, shared a manner of interacting with physical objects. It was immediate and impulsive; an object would have to move to them, not them to it. To be handled by one of Rhian's aunts was to be graunched and broken. Dismantled. Even Rhian sometimes found it difficult to stay whole around them. Gwen could sense even mild misery in just the rhythm of Rhian's breath. It wasn't that they picked on weakness; they sought it out with their grotesquely well-meaning demands.

Rhian was singularly focussed on what she was doing but all the flour and sugar in the air kept making her cough. The bustling bosoms that raised her were slowly suffocating her. She was choking on the new voice that was rising in her throat. All Rhian wanted was a slightly different life. Just different, exactly like everyone else. Everyone needed a little rebellion, a small protest. She looked over at Alys, quietly collecting the pale, raw Welsh cakes at the other end of the table. Biding her time, as always.

'I think Mam will be happy when she sees what we've put together.'

'I heard Sally Morgan was... you know...'

'Mam's not going to bloody see it, is she?'

'You heard she was what?'

'No, Mam won't, but I know she'd like it.'

'You know… a "Lady of Llangollen".'

'She'll be brought down to see soon enough.'

'Well good for Sally Morgan, I say.'

Rhian concentrated on the sustaining rhythm of batter being beaten into submission. At least you were safe by the sink, she thought, safe in the kitchen. Safe from your own potential. You knew what to expect, even when your husband slammed your skull against the porcelain, like Sally Morgan's did.

Looking around at her aunts, Rhian knew she could not fool the fates forever. When her body had softened and bled and her pores opened up, its function began to change. Expectations seized up in her joints and the flexible fabric of potential tightened around her. She had heard two wails and the third would signal the finished transition to the next stage, the new generation with Esyllt at the helm. It would push Rhian into her daughter-bearing years, increasing the volume of the biological bomb that ticked at her from her aunts' mouths. Until her blood ran dry and the hunting stopped, because with the raw smell of it gone, mutton wasn't supposed to attract the wolves.

A sharp knock at the front door shocked Wendy into dropping her rolling pin onto Helen's foot and, with that blow, came the final yelp. It was softer and more wounded than the previous two. Rhian felt it deep within herself somewhere far away.

Without needing to be told, she went out into the hall to open the front door. Silhouetted in the bright light was her father, probably coming in for his cold cup of tea that never arrived, and behind him, the undertakers. Rhian led the small, solemn parade into the kitchen.

15

'Come in, come in!'

'She's upstairs ready.'

'Tea?'

'Sit down, sit down!'

'We've done her hair and dressed her.'

'Milk?'

'Have a slice of cake while you're here.'

'Eat, eat!'

'Sugar?'

The body planters had finally arrived; ready to put Nana back in the ground. They politely declined refreshments before going upstairs to collect her. Then they ceremonially processed her swollen, brittle body downstairs for the last time and took her straight out the front door, feet first. Following closely, the sisters dusted themselves down and headed one by one, in their long black dresses and tall black hats, down the frozen path to the chapel.

Rhian watched them from the doorway with her father. She watched with quiet hope as Alys, at the end of the line as always, slipped away to meet Sally Morgan at a different type of shrine, to receive a different type of sacrament.

James, in During

Elizabeth Pratt

From his third-floor apartment, James can hear the painters working. They work all day long now the weather is sunny. He can't focus on anything else but the clank and bang of the men treading on the scaffolding. Oddly, it's not irritating him nearly as much as he imagined it would. The painters told the building owner that they'd be 'in and out in a couple of days'. That was three months ago, and they have only recently started to work.

In the past weeks, there have been bouts of high wind. The scaffolding creaked against the building and unearthly moans of air came through the pipes that held up the paint-spattered boards. That was the worst, the low whistles and whale-song of the wind. James, desperate to sleep, tried not to think of spirits and the angry dead; they still echoed around him.

It is a good thing that the painters have started work, that there is some activity outside. James hears them call to one another sometimes, or detects music and the muffled chirps of a radio DJ. Aside from that, life seems to be standing still, but for once he doesn't feel alone. Everyone is shut in, everyone is going mental. They're calling it 'lockdown', as if they had all been found guilty and sentenced. Staring at the ceiling and trying to sleep, some nights, he thinks this isn't far from the truth of it. This feels like a punishment for crimes that everyone knew they were doing but didn't think they'd ever get *caught* doing. And yet, what kind of punishment?

The things that made him awkward and weird in the *Before* are normal now, in the *During*. People talk about concealing their faces as if it bothers them. James was relieved to hear that he'd be openly wearing a mask. Staying in has become something even popular people do. He doesn't have to make excuses for not seeing anyone.

He hesitates to call it a silver lining, because that's when people react badly to him. He tries not to say anything about it at all. He's found, on the inevitable work phone calls, that it is acceptable to make low, non-committal noises like small sighs or groans – sounds that could mean anything and are interpreted into whatever the listener wants to hear.

'I'll miss my granddaughter's third birthday,' a co-worker complains. James groans. His colleague says, 'I know. Awful thing, this.'

It saves a lot of needless talk.

**

It's been three months and James has been the happiest he can remember. No, not about all those things on the news; not the crying nurses, the exhausted medical staff, the virtual and video funerals. Who would take delight in that? He has compassion. He's not a psychopath.

It's more the empty streets and return of birdsong, the blank blue sky and absence of contrails. The way that delivery people step far back from his door and call to him from the stairwell, unseen. Shopping online is preferable, of course; there is no pressure from bullying salespeople. He doesn't miss fitting rooms, with their thin curtains and contorting mirrors. He certainly doesn't wish to use a self-checkout ever again.

But he is *enjoying* it, and that feels wrong.

It's this: he finally has the time to do whatever he wants. He's watching TED talks, learning two languages, cooking (once he managed to get some groceries in). He's studying and reading more than he's managed in the last four years. He's happy – goddammit, he'll just say it: he's content.

And the apartments around his are quiet. His elderly neighbour, Mrs Givens, was moved out by her daughter (in violation of hastily-enacted law) to go and live in Surrey. James didn't envy Mrs Givens. She hadn't been a loud neighbour – though the telly was cranked up – but she was often confused and sang to herself, no matter what the time, and James found the randomness of it slightly upsetting. He wonders whether, in this new world, he'll come to miss her. Will he miss hearing the breathless canting of songs from the 40s – a hit parade of wartime jingles? She was stuck in that era, though she couldn't have been more than a child during the war. Perhaps, James thinks, that's why she's gone back to it: it was a time when everybody was expected to take care of her.

On the other side lives a young woman who writes for some online financial news-page. James imagines she's been so busy with her work that she doesn't have time to make much noise. He hasn't seen her in two months, not since an awkward encounter on the staircase when he backed up the stairs hurriedly as if she had plague. They did a shuffle, a weird dance that eventually made them both laugh. His laugh was a snort behind his mask and he worried she thought he was huffing in contempt. It bothered him for hours afterward.

It's not as though they spoke much *Before*, and he was baffled as to why he cared what she thought of his behaviour that day. He thought about it and decided she represented

Everyone Else. He's not concerned with social faux pas, simply curious, as if *Everyone Else* is a different animal in the same park. He wants to figure out his place, his role. He's even been taking online psychology courses and learning how to manage anxiety, his own and other people's. The courses were two-for-one.

Some of the behaviours he's seen on the news, and down below on the street, confirm what James has often considered: people are the worst. People are undisciplined, selfish, violent animals who so often fail to access their higher brain functions. Capable of so much more, and yet always repeating mistakes and never seeming to learn. He doesn't want to be part of that; he doesn't want to be associated with them. It feels natural now to refer to humans in the third person. As he stares at the ceiling of his bedroom, he thinks about this. *Where does that leave me, then? What species do I belong with?*

And mostly he thinks, *How do I get home?*

**

In the fourth month, James has a call from his Aunt Lydia in Stafford. He hasn't spoken to her for more than five years, not since his mother's wake. He thinks back on the day and it brings no other memory to mind – no sadness, not even a sting of grief. Remembering the buffet line, though, brings painful memories of pasta salad and room-temperature meats. It was bothersome on the day and it still is. But his aunt is on the phone and saying something, repeating herself because she sounds annoyed.

'Isn't that awful?' she says. 'Those people! The lot of them want shot.'

He makes a throat noise, a kind of grunt. He has the lost power of speech.

'I suppose it's alright for you, down there,' she says.

Down there. She's right. He is in some kind of hole. He imagines looking up at her round face and crooked eyebrows, the powder-puff circles of blusher on yellowing skin. She has been unhealthy all of her life, but it was her sister who died. *One-in-six have a bad reaction to life.*

Did he giggle? He clears his throat.

Aunt Lydia gives local news. Not a word of catching up, no attempt to ask about his situation. James supposes that she has worked her way through her contacts and is only calling him because everyone else has told her to bugger off. She as much as says so: 'I'm reaching out because it's important to be close to family.'

Reaching out. She's been binge-watching some terrible American police dramas. *Well, why not? Hasn't he been catering to base behaviours, too?*

'Family,' he says, finally. 'Important.'

'Yes. And your mother would want to know I'm watching out for you.'

He sees her at the edge, again. Reaching a fat arm to him, not in a real effort to make contact, just holding it there, in the circle of light at the top of the hole, waving to him. Her arm is freckled from too much sun.

The thought of sunlight, and his throat catches. He coughs around it.

'My god, you haven't got it?' she says.

'Got it?'

'Our Geoff got it at the take-away,' she says. 'He was safe in the pub, but the government wouldn't let him eat there. See where it gets us?'

He has no words. He holds his phone away from his ear

and squints at it, taps the red receiver icon. Wonders why that is the icon for a phone call when half the people have never seen a phone receiver.

That night, he turns off his phone and puts it in a jar of rice. He doesn't know why.

**

Friday the… ?th.

At management request, he drags out an aged computer and sets up some virtual boardroom app. The PC is grindingly slow and has no camera. He's grateful the HR woman can't see his expression. She interviewed him in person three years ago and now brings the virtual bad news: *unprecedented times*, she says, but there's nothing new about getting the sack.

James gets caught up in a whirlpool of search terms and the history of labour disputes. It's less interesting than he'd imagined.

**

Tuesday, or maybe Thursday, the woman next door is on the stairs, bringing up bags of shopping strung along a broom handle. He was coming back from a walk – he walks, now, because his ankles are swelling up from immobility – and saw her ahead of him, moving up the stairs. He stood in the foyer and waited for her to get a head start, standing back with his hands folded as if in respect for the dead. From somewhere, he found his manners and called up the stairs, 'Do you need help? I can help.' His voice croaked from disuse and made him sound as if he were ill. Cringing, he added, 'I'm not ill.'

Which made it even worse.

No wonder she didn't answer.

22

At 1:39 in the morning, his bedroom ceiling is a collage of colours from chargers and devices that surround his life. There is no real pattern to the Artex; the ceiling looks like the surface of the moon. He thinks about the coldness of space, the silence. How would he do, up there in a capsule, some kind of Major Tom figure, utterly alone? Unable to get out... would it be so different?

It would. He should be grateful to have what freedom of movement he manages. His walks are never long, just the fifteen minutes and half of that is getting ready to leave the airlock of his flat. Mask, keys, gloves, hat. Checking his courier bag – he refuses to call it a 'man-bag' as that phrase makes him think of a scrotum – for sanitiser and alcohol wipes. He has a keyring trademarked 'The Germinator', a crude-looking hook and probe that is meant to prevent the need to touch door handles and lift buttons. It doesn't work properly. He keeps it with him at all times. By the time he gets out of the flat and onto the stairs, he feels drained of what energy he thought he had. He's committed by then. He carries on, and some days just the walk down the stairs and back up again is deemed to be sufficient. He has become a kind of GP of his own, with all the googling he does about ailments.

It used to be the symptoms of The Virus, but now, if anything seems amiss, he searches terms: *Palpitations. Night sweats. Dry mouth. Why is my hair falling out?* He never looks up *Insomnia* – he takes that as normal, now. He contemplated pills, but isn't he dulled enough?

**

23

At the beginning of December, he accidentally picks up post meant for the woman next door. He assumes she is Rachel. It looks to be some hand-delivered card and not particularly well-sealed. He could open it if he wanted, just have a glance at the message. Something about Christmas wishes, doubtless, but as he hasn't got even a card from Aunt Lydia he might enjoy reading the greeting. He could pretend for a moment it was meant for him.

The envelope remains sealed and he thinks about how best to get it to her. He could put it under the door, but she might miss it. It could go under a hallway rug or get thrown away with the endless flyers for the Pizza Factory that keep showing up. No, he'll have to hand it to her.

It doesn't occur to him to put it back where he found it – that would mean taking exercise outside of his scheduled walk. He sets the card on the hallway table, propped up by a bottle of sanitiser, where he can see it.

**

It might be the 10th of December. He hasn't checked. Somewhere in the middle of the month, and people are talking on the news about going to see their families. It's incomprehensible to James, all this talk about gathering. They have access to health reports and updates; why is there a question? When will it sink in?

James likes to imagine that Rachel will stay in the building for the holidays. Her door hasn't been decorated, as some in the building have been. One person has wrapped their door entirely in kitchen foil and crossed it with a yellow bow. He supposes it's meant to be a present, a gift to all. To James, it looks very much like crime-scene tape. He can only imagine the gory scene on the other side of the door: *bloody handprints,*

24

a knife missing from a kitchen block. A bathtub full of acid wash.
He shakes the thought from his head as soon as he is able, but
the images linger.

**

Not every person is having a hard time. Perhaps Rachel is
fine, keeping a tidy flat and occasionally treating herself to
throw-cushions in neutral colours: caramel, oatmeal, mocha,
a daring dash of burnt carrot. When he brings the card to her,
will he get to see into her flat? Or will she keep the door
opened only a fraction, holding it in place with her hip? He
pictures her in leggings and an oversized cardigan.
Something cosy. Maybe fluffy woollen socks, though they
would slip on a parquet floor. She seems too sensible to risk
injury for comfort – she wears her mask just to go down to
pick up packages.

She might not even open the door but call out for him to
leave the card on the floor. That would be best, but the
thought that she wouldn't open the door sparks a sliver of
irritation in him. *I've been staying in. She knows that, she must.
Why would she assume I'm infected? I've been careful.*

It takes another day of deliberation before he is ready to
go over.

**

It's around seven in the evening. He should have thought it
through, because he can smell cooking in the hallway and not
everyone has given up mealtimes. It smells good, too,
something rich. A bolognese, a beef stew. He stands still for a
moment and closes his eyes, trying to remember the last time
he ate a meal with someone else. He counts even strangers,

25

but he can't remember how long it's been. Something about the smell of cooking makes his eyes well up. He swallows back saliva, pulls himself together.

When he turns the card in his hands, he is gratified to see there is no message on the envelope. No stamp, of course, but who sends letters and cards nowadays, even *Before*? The card seems cheap, too; it's poor paper stock and the envelope is thin enough to make out some detail: red, a Santa hat? Possibly the orange of a snowman carrot. He turns the envelope over and looks at the writing on the front: *Rachel Hagen*. No more, nothing he can work with. Ink of a fountain pen, not a biro. A woman, then. This clue gives him a trickle of what must be pleasure.

He shouldn't interrupt her dinner. He's not that sort of person.

He returns to his flat, quiet as can be.

**

Her name is definitely Rachel. He's checked and checked again. Using Christian names is very forward, even now. He'll call her Miss Hagen. No, wait: *Miz*. In the black and white films he's been watching, this address is given with a drawl and a tipped cowboy hat. James hasn't the head for hats; his father left when James was nine, but managed to impart that wisdom somewhere in those early years.

A scarf, then, just to draw attention to the fact that he's bothered to shave. Steady hands, few nicks, pale mask of his once-beard now obvious, making his face look divided. It wasn't much of a beard, but it has a ghost. He'll have to wait until it evens out.

There's nothing he can do about his hair; he'd only make it worse.

**

On Sunday, he realises he has not heard church bells for almost a year. So many noises have fallen away. He wishes Mrs Givens would sing something; only later, he remembers she is gone. The building seems to be emptying out, but he never sees people actually leaving. It's as if they fade out and take their noises with them.

The quiet amplifies everything else. At 3:17 one morning, he hears bottles clanking down the rubbish chute at the end of the hallway. The hatch is outside Rachel's flat. He stays awake, alert, and pulls the pillow over his head when he hears what sounds like sobbing.

It is unbearable.

**

Hallway. A very cold day in December. The heating wafts through vents and sounds as though the building is breathing. James focusses on her door, notes the crumpled flyer that has not made it past the letterbox brushes. *Who is bringing these things?*

He considers leaving the card, tilted against the door. He'll knock to let her know it's there. Or not. She'll see it when next she leaves, won't she? He doesn't want to frighten her, standing there and blocking the only exit of her home. No, he'll leave it and be done with it.

Hesitation is the worst. What if she needs help?

What if he is too late to help?

She may be in the bed, or on the floor, limbs stiff with thickened blood. It could be over already. A broken wine bottle, a bedside table peppered with tablets. A bathtub full of ribboned water —

No.

Everyone is trying to live through it. Nobody wants to leave halfway through; but there is no timeline and no ending in sight. That could drive a person to desperate measures.

The Three Fates. Spinning, measuring, cutting.

Back in his flat, card on the table, he googles it: the Fates have names, too. He finds out this trivia and resents that he has no-one to tell.

**

He's opened the card. Half a bottle of something disgusting that he thought he'd cook with, and then he was devil-may-care. Ripped the envelope with clumsy fingers and the card slid out easily.

Outside, a robin atop a post-box, colour against the backdrop of pristine snow.

Inside, a message: *Ray: So sorry to say that Grandpa Burt has passed away. It was peaceful.*

James feels sick; it's too late to take it back.

He has secret knowledge that must be shared.

Oh, no.

**

8:15 one morning, the window washer uses the scaffolding to make his job easier. Yes, it is still up. Nobody finds it odd that the washer walks along the warped boards and peers into the flats where the curtains are open. A lot of people have left, gone on to live within a bubble or country house. If they can afford rent in this city, they can afford something else. Anything else.

James doesn't know why he stays.

He remains in bed for most of the mornings and some of the afternoons. It's getting harder to get up and move about when there's nowhere to go. Through the blackout curtains – life during wartime – he hears the washer pause, bucket clanking as he rests it on the boards. *Why is he stopping? Chalking the wall, letting others of the criminal ilk know the flat seems empty. The fraternity. The brotherhood of cat burglars.*

James wonders if they can still be called 'cat burglars' when there is no prowess involved. They would simply climb the scaffolding and kick in the window. Not very debonair, but it gets the job done. *The Window Kickers' Club.*

He's not overly worried about it.

He has nothing to steal.

**

The weird displacement of time makes it difficult to judge when Rachel might reasonably be awake. If she's anything like James, even on a species level, she is keeping odd hours. For his own amusement (who else has he got to amuse?), he's been thinking of things in very technical or Austin-esque terms. The pain of toothache becomes 'oral discomfort', the crescent-moon burn on his forearm, from the new wok, becomes 'a thermal, dermal reaction'.

Very technically, then, last night Rachel was excreting excess neurosynaptic stimulus. In other words, shriek-sobbing.

He wonders if she has already learned about Grandpa Burt, or if it's just everything else. Every single other thing else.

Who is he to add to that? Maybe he should destroy the card. He could shred it with all the pizza palace flyers and free newspapers, and stuff a pillowcase.

A recycled-media domestic comfort item.

And then, as has been happening a lot lately, his mind hop-skips ahead: setting up the home office so Rachel can work the last month of her pregnancy from their home. Such a luxury not to have to go into the office, the novelty of it amuses them. He lifts the box of stationery for her – he doesn't have to, she's perfectly *capable* – but he wants to care for her, for their child. He bought her a plant to set on the corner, something living to bring a good energy to the space.

She tells him, then, that she can feel the baby kicking. She doesn't need more than that.

(Too late, now. He's spoiled it. Says, before he can stop himself, *'What about me? Don't you need me?'* And his amazing, beautiful, too-good-for-him wife gives him a pitying look.)

He's taken the dream too far. He tries to go back, he still can, *'Remember when we first met?'*

And he rewrites it from there, because he can. There is still a future.

**

Day 6 of Knowing About Burt.

His palms are always damp, now. He went through a bit where he thought he had a fever, sweating sickness and disease through every pore. In bed, that horrible, cratered ceiling, and he ran through everywhere he'd been, everything outside that he touched. A bench, without thinking. The door latch, his keys. He slipped up, forgot to picture everything covered in the fluorescent paint of virus, contaminants all around him. He chewed his thumbnail down to the quick and knows it got in him that way, and now it's ripping through his bloodstream and webbing in his lung tissue. He could be dead within days.

30

My god, he's boiling alive. Fevered and strange, his mind wanders.

They have a son, Ethan. Somehow, they stay together but Rachel is working long hours and it's down to James to pick the boy up from school. Their boy is clever, but not adjusting socially. No-one is overly concerned, not yet. *He gets it from his father*, Rachel says. She's affectionate with it, this time. *It took two years of living next door to me before he introduced himself.*

Two years and sixty-three days.

He'll never know, now. He's got this thing and it will ravage him, tear down the structure of his innards and he'll die, there on the gurney in the corridor. The nurses will be harassed and hurried. It will take three hours to notice he's gone.

Dry-land drowned.

3:17 am:
False alarm. The thermostat was broken.
His temperature is a smidge under 37C.

**

He cannot
cannot
cannot
take it.

**

The 28th Day of December.
He doesn't know where he finds it, the courage. But he drags it from the depth, like a golden Roman trinket dredged from greasy clay. Nevermind, he finds it. That's enough.

Three knocks (one too few, she would miss it, four too insistent and intrusive) and he jogs away, a good eighteen feet away, and he's wearing two masks.

He will not turn away until she opens the door, and when she does, he cannot see her. 'I'm here,' he calls, and she leans her head out, looks the wrong way, then to him.

'Hello, neighbour,' he says. Behind his mask, he smiles.

She's wearing glasses. Blinks at him, confused. 'Uh, hi.' Her hair is neat, combed back, sleek. She's wearing a nice blouse and pyjama bottoms. Barefoot. Barefaced.

He imagines a thought bubble appearing above him, graphic novel text – Do Not Objectify Her. He's never been happier to see anybody.

'There was a card,' he begins, 'a few days ago, a week. Two weeks.' *Get to the point.* 'I thought it might be for me. I just – yeah, no. It's for you. I opened it by mistake.'

She shakes her head, puzzled, half-smiling. 'Uh, okay. That's okay.' She bends down, picks up the card. Reads it and her smile fades. She nods.

'I'm really sorry about your grandpa—' he says. Then, 'I didn't mean to read it, though.'

'He was a German Shepherd,' she says. 'Sixteen years old, poor thing. My sister's dog.'

Inexplicably, this seems much sadder to him. 'Oh, no. I should have brought it over right away. I wanted to. I just couldn't. Sometimes I can't move.'

'No, I get it.' Her smile is faint, but there. She is out of habit. 'Truth is, you're just in time,' she says.

It's something in the tone. He wants her to know he noticed. He starts to turn away, stops. In the dim corridor, they stare at each other.

'I know exactly what you mean,' James says.

Rachel nods, and opens her door just a little bit more.

Conditions for an Avalanche

Kate Lockwood Jefford

All an avalanche requires is a mass of snow and a slope for it to slide down.

She breathes in. She breathes out. She's been in her studio for the hours since he left. Warm fingers working cold, damp clay the colour of toffee. Softening, shaping, sculpting from the images in her head. Images that refuse to fade. Her hands feel grainy.

Now, in her kitchen, all she wants is to slip off her chair into a heap of herself. She presses hard on the soles of her slipper feet – these days always slipper feet – and sits and waits.

Sits and waits.

He gets back from his shift at 10.15 a.m. Any later and her mind mangles itself around all manner of accidents waiting to happen in a warehouse. Towering structures teetering. Toppling. It only takes a breeze, a knock, a nudge. Objects can dislodge, slip and slide and fall. Suffocating, body-crushing, skull-splitting objects.

She hopes he'd have his wits about him and run.

She can't lose him too.

She focusses on the wall ahead, on the acoustic guitar hanging there. Tooth-white tuning keys. Long, tapered mahogany neck criss-crossed with strings and frets. The polished curves of its cedarwood waist and body, the bridge and pickguard she helped him paint gold.

She hears the door, the blast of irate traffic, and he comes in bringing a whiff of diesel fumes and damp air. A plaster on his thumb. A blue plaster. The thumb on his left hand. His fretting hand.

Cardboard cut, he says.

He can't be bothered with the blue protective gloves they issue. Too much faff pulling them on and off what with all the hydraulic controls, the levers and gears and steering, lifting and lowering and tilting, corkscrewing his neck to drive the forklift up and down and round the twenty-two lanes linking collection, storage and despatch interface stations.

He gets splinters from the palettes too. The last one got infected and he wouldn't go to the doctor.

He holds up his plastered thumb like a thumbs-up okay cool sign.

It bled and bled, he says. So much fucking blood.

Did you have a tourniquet? she says.

When she slices her own thumb – peeling or chopping or checking she's alive – she uses one of those rubber bands the post comes bound in. She keeps them in her cutlery drawer, hundreds of them, like little loops of blue liquorice. Sometimes she imagines lying down in her cutlery drawer in a special groove carved for a Thumbelina version of herself. Sliding into the dark.

He doesn't answer the tourniquet question. She's not surprised. Working six-hour stretches at a time in that place: a blue box with corrugated metal walls high as any cathedral, a floor the size of forty football pitches. A colossal echo-chamber of clanking and clattering, whirring and whining, thudding and scraping and slamming as load after load after

34

load of palleted flatpacks wrapped in acres of plastic is shifted in and shifted out.

He doesn't wear the blue protective ear plugs either.

And he has to crease and fold and sardine his beanpole body into a cab the size of a dodgem's.

He's storing up trouble for his back.

He gets paid a little more since doing the forklift training.

He hasn't paid the electricity bill on his flat around the corner. The flat where he's lived alone since dropping out of Uni. The flat she's never seen because he doesn't want her to. They've already threatened to cut him off and if they do there'll be court costs to pay on top, and then what?

He's been staying in the back room, the room that used to be his brother's. He can't give up his flat and move in officially because they'd cut her benefits and he can't pay her what she'd lose.

His car needs an MOT that it won't pass and he can't afford the repairs.

With no car he'd have to walk the five miles to work as there are no buses at 4 a.m.

And he's never taken a taxi in his life.

The slope must be shallow enough for snow to accumulate but steep enough for it to accelerate. Typically, slab avalanches occur on slopes of 30 to 50 degrees.

They sit at her kitchen table. A family table. A table that seats four though it's rarely more than two now.

Him and her. Small faces, pinched and pale as the rain sliding down her windows. Eyes mere dots of dilute blue.

Indoor faces.

She used to look younger than she is.

People would say they could be brother and sister.

Sometimes her sister comes with wine and chat. The chat runs out before the wine, her sister's voice flagging as she tries to keep it light. She never touches the fat glass of red or white or whatever her sister pours for her. If she started, she wouldn't stop until she could pour herself back into the bottle.

She can't go down that route again.

Her sister always leaves the unfinished bottle. Sometimes she thinks of using it to make a pasta sauce. But she hasn't cooked food like that in ages.

A slurry of shame oozes from the cracks inside her. She imagines disassembling her body and compressing it into a flatpack. Encased in cardboard. Fork-lifted. Slotted onto a high shelf.

The size of an avalanche ranges from a small shifting of loose snow (sloughing) to the displacement of enormous slabs of snow.

One half of the table is taken up with her purse, her pouch of tobacco, her phone, his phone, her keys, his keys. A pile of post. Letters from the department of work and pensions. The community mental health team. A disabled bus-pass application form she can't face filling in. Her keyworker says she's eligible on account of the meds. She can't imagine ever getting on a bus again. All those people. All those pairs of eyes. Nowhere to hide.

There's also an unopened envelope. Her name on it. His writing.

Inside, she knows, is a £10 note. The £10 he owes her. The £10 she gave him for petrol, that she's told him he can keep, she doesn't want back.

The £10 he won't accept.

It stays there. Unopened. Unspoken.

There is so much to not talk about.

They stare in silence at different dusty corners of the room. Dust trodden in on shoes and boots, dust from soil and pollen and grit and microscopic bits of plastic. Dust sloughed off skin and hair and nails, fibres shed from jeans and shirts and hoodies.

When they're gone, dust is all that's left.

All she has to keep them close.

Once snow is on the ground, the ice crystals undergo physical changes that differentiate layers deeper in the snowpack from those on top and may weaken the layers beneath a cohesive slab of snow which fractures and starts to slide.

Last night he slept in his blue work overalls on the sofa so it was easier to get up to clock in for his 4 a.m. shift. It's always harder after a few days off. He always tries to be quiet. She always hears. The click of the front door closing behind him is her signal to swing her legs out of bed, slide her feet into her slippers, unlock the door to her studio.

She asks if he's had any breakfast. He says the canteen staff start their shift half an hour later so there's no breakfast ready for the night shift. He says breakfast is not a priority. She makes him a cup of milky tea with four sugars. Baby tea.

The edges of his plaster are already frayed. His hair is overgrown and his chin looks grubby. She hopes he's not growing a beard again, wishes he'd shave so his face was silky-smooth and cute again. Wishes he'd get a proper haircut and not do it himself with two mirrors and the kitchen scissors. Wishes his clothes didn't hang off him like washing on a line on a windless day.

She wears the same black jeans and black jumper she's worn all week.

She'd once put on a red silk polka-dot dress to see him

play. A proud front-row dress. He stood tall on stage in a jade and black diamond-patterned shirt with a silver thread woven through.

The dress hangs half-forgotten and faceless in the darkness of her wardrobe.

He doesn't play the guitar anymore. Doesn't write songs with hope strung through the chords. Lilting in the lyrics.

On his days off he buys clapped-out guitars off the internet, rebuilds and re-conditions, restrings and retunes, polishes and paints. Hangs them on the walls.

When people want to buy them for £300, £500, £1000 and more, he says they're not for sale.

When he is offered money to play, he says no.

Once the conditions for an avalanche exist, a trigger simply applies sufficient force to release it.

She'd once sat in a bar in Seville sipping chilled Oloroso, sheltering from soft warm afternoon rain, gazing at a double-height wall covered with framed monochrome photographs of guitars in all stages of being made. She'd taken photos with her phone and tried to send them to his email but it didn't work. He didn't receive them.

She's got everything wrong with him, with his brother too.

She breathes out, she breathes in. Her kitchen smells of grime and grease, stale dishcloth and potatoes on the turn. Rainwater drips from a spot on the ceiling into the family-sized ice-cream tub she found when she was looking for the bucket. She tries to ignore it so her mind doesn't latch onto all the jobs lining up in the house. The holes and cracks and things come loose. The jobs that can't be done until the weather improves and who would do them anyway even if she could afford to pay.

And she can't imagine inflating her lungs and getting herself to all her appointments, can't imagine taking all the pills boxed up on the shelf next to where she keeps the tea. The ones for unbidden thoughts, the ones for the side-effects of the ones for unbidden thoughts, the ones for blood pressure. For anaemia. Constipation.

She wants to raise her arm and sweep the boxes to the floor.

She wants to put on her leather-palm gloves and safety goggles, shut herself in her studio with a fresh slab of black wax.

90% of people who die in avalanches trigger them themselves.

He tells her it was raining in the warehouse last night. Inside. Puddles everywhere, he says, buckets dotted about. Buckets he couldn't see from the cab as he drove up and down the drenched aisles cornering, swivelling, reversing. So distracted he was, he says, by the rain falling on him and the truck, he drove the mast into a metal beam. Dented it. He had to file an incident report. They had to close off the whole section because the upper bay of an entire aisle storing flat-packed furniture was unsafe.

There could've been an avalanche of wardrobes, he says. *Avalanche.*

They both know this is a word he didn't mean to say.

He's already had a written warning for lateness and other incidents, and if he loses his job, what then?

A pause. The plip-plop of water like a countdown.

She hears the scrape of his chair, his boots on the stairs, the bang of the back-room door. She must have said all that out loud.

People usually die from asphyxia due to lack of oxygen when buried in snow, rather than blunt trauma or hypothermia.

She breathes in, breathes out, pushes her shoulder blades down her back, pulls her elbows in, draws a circle in the air with her nose, one way, and the other. Feels her neck crunch. She presses on the soles of her slipper feet, forces herself to stand and wash the teacups.

Balanced on the rim of the boiler above the sink is a picture, a Kodachrome snapshot of a family: mother, father, two sons. Tanned, glowing skin, eyes big and blue as the Alpine sky behind them.

Outdoor faces.

A picture taken a year before her younger son didn't return from snowboarding on a black run.

There were reports of an avalanche.

The post-mortem concluded he was hit by a large piece of frozen snow and died immediately at the scene from his injuries.

She goes upstairs, opens the door to the back room where her son lies on his front, asleep in his blue warehouse overalls. It looks as though someone is next to him, hidden in the fat folds of duvet beneath his flung-out arm. His left arm. His fretting arm.

She lifts the duvet and sees a guitar, his arm resting across its waist, his fingers on its neck lying next to his on the pillow.

There was a girl, once. A meeting online. Mutual friends. Musical connections. Anticipation, excitement. A car journey. A long walk, the pub, a take-away. A bounce in his voice when she'd called him to see how it went.

A-dor-able she was, he'd said. *A-dor-able.*

Only he didn't hear from her again. He waited. And waited. Nothing.

How can people do that to people?

Their father was a musician. She thought he'd be better with grief. Not a man who told her she'd gone cold. A man who left.

She unlocks the door to her studio, a box room she's painted blue, puts on her leather-palm gloves and safety goggles, severs a slice from her new slab of black wax with her soldering iron. Melts it in the slow-cooker. It'll take hours yet to create a mould. Another day dipping in silicone slurry to build a ceramic shell. Layer by layer. Half an inch thick. Several more hours in the kiln to lose the wax and bake the shell, turning it from pale yellow to the colour of dirty snow.

When the shell is hard and dry, she will stand on a ladder to place it – as precariously as she can – on the high shelf that runs around the room.

Her sister is pushing her to have the pieces cast in shining aluminium. To show and sell. People will love them, she says. Her sister thinks they are abstract.

Only she knows they are pieces of frozen snow.

Coat of Arms

Craig Hawes

Ellis had gone mad for all things medieval since Vincent Parry's phone call three weeks ago and already I was yearning for the return of his dinosaur phase.

First there were the imaginary arrows shot at passing cars on the school run every morning (I say 'shot'; Ellis was quick to inform me that the correct term was 'loosed'). Then I discovered he'd been using my fishing rod as a lance, charging down the street on his BMX and using the 'For Sale' sign in front of Mrs Morgan's bungalow as target practice so that it now looked as though it had been freckled with bullet holes.

'That boy of yours needs a firm hand,' she'd said when I popped round to apologise.

'Granted, but he's been through a lot this year,' I'd replied, at which she had knowingly nodded and offered her own apology.

Another time, I had walked into the garden one afternoon to find what appeared to be a wonky letter *O* the size of a bicycle-wheel gouged into the baize-like perfection of the lawn.

'Ellis?' I'd said, fighting to rein in my exasperation. 'Is this some sort of weird flowerbed? Because you *really* should have asked me first.'

'No, Dad. Like, duh! It's a moat for my Lego castle.'

We'd ended up finishing the job together, working well into the evening with earth under our fingernails and grass stains on our knees as we filled it with water and — my idea — a floating armada of miniature plastic crocodiles.

'You do know they didn't have crocodiles in medieval Wales, right Dad?' he'd said. 'It's kind of unrealistic.'

With each misdemeanour I chose to praise his creativity rather than scold him. Since Kirsten — his mother, my ex-wife — died a year ago, I've taken a laissez-faire approach to discipline. And in any case, Ellis is a sensitive kid. The kind where the waterworks come a little too easily, and whom you worry about finding his groove in a cruel world. The time for tough love lay somewhere in the future.

As for Vincent Parry, I'd been expecting him to get in touch for some time, wondered what was taking him so long. And then one Friday evening, after I'd bathed Ellis and put him to bed, he'd rung me.

I was in the kitchen doing the washing-up and I'd instantly recognised the number on my screen.

'Nick. It's me, Vince,' he'd said, needlessly. 'Just calling to see how Ellis is doing. I know it's been a while but I thought I'd let things settle down first.'

'He's fine,' I replied. 'Enjoying his new school, making friends.'

'That's good, I knew he would.'

'Yeah.'

'He's a great kid.'

'He is.'

'I really miss him.'

'And what about you, Vince? How are you coping?'

'I'm… getting there.'

Hearing the clink of colliding ice cubes and maudlin music playing low in the background, I felt a pang of pity for Vince, who according to one mutual friend had taken to leaving a single red rose on Kirsten's grave every day. And I considered raising the idea of him seeing Ellis sometime, which I felt was the reason he was calling me anyway.

I had always known that he'd want to reconnect with him at some point. He and Kirsten had been living together in Bristol for three years before she passed away, during which he had spent far more time with my son than I had. When Kirsten died, Ellis had come to live with me; there was never any question of him living with Vince. As Vince and Kirsten had never actually married, he wasn't even Ellis's official step-father. Grudgingly, however, I had accepted that a bond had formed between them and I had no intention of breaking it.

Still, I wasn't going to go out of my way to facilitate any reunion, either. There had been friction between Vince and I in the past — a 'cessation of niceties', as I had referred to it at the time — that stemmed from some trivial and long-forgotten dispute.

This in turn had led to he and I grappling each other to the floor in the rain-soaked car park of a service station off the M4 one Sunday night after I'd delivered Ellis back to his mother. An undignified scene for anyone, let alone two men at the threshold of middle age, both of whom were carrying some excess timber around the midriff — me by a plank or two, Vince by a log-cabin. Insults had been traded in the run-up to this unedifying skirmish, juvenile stuff that had triggered a ripple of sniggers among the people queuing outside Greggs.

Vince, who as the accounts manager of an office furniture factory was hardly a reservoir of originality, had labelled me 'a first-rate wanker', whereas I had countered with 'Go fuck yourself, rainbow Zeppelin!' A cruel dig at his ample girth and Hawaiian shirt, of which he seemed to own an inexhaustible collection.

Breaking up the fight — if you could even call it that — Kirsten had denounced the pair of us as 'macho imbeciles' and made us shake hands. Ellis, to my shame, had witnessed the whole thing from the rear seat of Vince's Nissan Juke.

'Does he talk about Kirsten much?' Vince said, breaking the silence now.

'Yeah, all the time.'

'I found some old photos of her the other day. Can I send them to him?'

'That's kind of you, yeah.'

'And I was, uh... I was wondering if I could maybe see him some time?'

Finally, he'd got to the point.

'Yeah, I'm sure we can arrange something,' I said. 'One of these days.'

'I've joined a medieval re-enactment society,' he said.

'Oh? Sounds interesting,' I said, thrown off-guard by what appeared to be an abrupt deviation in topic.

'Yeah, I felt like I needed a hobby to take my mind off everything. And this bloke in my bereavement group invited me along one day. I got really into it and the rest, as they say, is history.'

'Ha! Good one,' I said, certain that he had used that line before.

'Well, anyway, there's an event at Margam Park on Bank Holiday Monday where we're putting on a few things. Jousting displays, fun stuff for the kids. I was thinking Ellis could come. It's down the road from you.'

'Right. The thing is....'

'Come on, mate. Bet you could do with a break.'

'The thing is, you'd be taking part in this war stuff and...'

45

'Re-enactment. *Medieval* re-enactment.'

'Re-enactment, right. So I'm just wondering how you're gonna look after Ellis when you're playing bows and arrows.'

I heard a deep intake of breath and something — a whisky tumbler, perhaps — being set down without delicacy on a hard surface.

'Look, Nick, I'd be standing around mostly. I'd be able to keep my eye on him.'

'I don't know, Vince. All those crowds.'

'Well... you could come too, I suppose. It might be fun.'

At this point I could have said no, suggested he take him out some other time. But maybe I wanted to get it out of the way for another six months, or whatever frequency he assumed he was going to be seeing Ellis from now on. This was unlikely to be a one-off. Was this man now going to be in our lives forever? The idea that I might be setting a precedent made me feel uneasy.

A carousel of future scenarios revolved before my mind's eye: Vince and I stood shoulder-to-shoulder on the touchline as Ellis made his debut for the school rugby team; Vince and I collecting him at the airport as he returned home, tanned and tattooed, from a gap-year in South America; and both of us — by now haggard and hunchbacked — tossing confetti over Ellis and his bride at the church gates.

And so on, and so forth, through the decades, until death do us part.

I couldn't see Vince as anything more than a tiresome burden, an albatross around my neck. And yet, despite this, there was a tiny, vindictive part of me that was desperate to see him make a fool of himself at this medieval circus. Wanted Ellis to see it too. So easy to imagine him clanking around some boggy field in a suit of armour, looking less like Ivanhoe and more like the Tin Man from *The Wizard of Oz*.

Vince was right, it might be fun. It might be fucking hilarious.

'Okay, fine,' I said, taking a bottle of beer out of the fridge. 'We'll both come. It'll be nice for you to spend some time with him.'

'Really? Nice one, Nick, I'd love that!'

He went over some details — the date, the times — and I made a note on the jotter pad stuck to the fridge door.

'One last thing,' I said. 'We don't need to wear fancy dress, do we?'

I sensed a roll of the eyes as he said, 'For god's sake, Nick, it's not cosplay!'

**

The day of the event was a sticky, late-summer scorcher, the vapour trails from jet planes strung across the blue expanse of the sky like frayed ropes. We arrived mid-morning and after finding a parking space I slathered factor 50 over Ellis's arms, legs and face.

We headed towards the main grounds, set before the castle, which was hardly a castle at all, really. Straight out of the pages of a Wilkie Collins ghost story, this dank-looking country house had never been pounded by the battering rams of siege warfare, but if this registered with Ellis, by now a bottomless well of medieval wisdom, he was too polite to point it out.

A cluster of white marquee tents inched into view as we got closer, the crowds thickening. We passed a couple of ponies munching grass beneath three poles bearing heraldic flags that hung forlornly in the still air. From somewhere I caught the throat-burning whiff of charred meat, perhaps a boar roasting on a spit.

Briefly, we stopped at a large table displaying a cornucopia of armour and weapons. There were swords, knives, an iron mace and what looked like a pair of oversized spiky testicles on a chain. Slipping on a chainmail glove, I flinched at the feel of its fabric lining, moistened by the sweat of strangers.

A section of pathway in front of the castle was lined with stalls selling everything from toy swords to medieval books. One was run by a young woman who, for a small fee, offered to design your own bespoke coat of arms. Ellis nagged me to get one done but I told him we'd come back later, certain he'd forget about it by home time.

Eventually we came to a large area cordoned off by rope where two knights were engaged in battle, the clang and rasp of their swords mingling with the low hum of a food stall's electric generator. Their helmets looked like cylindrical bins with a horizontal slit at eye level and they had different shields to tell them apart – one with a silver dragon on a blue background, the other bearing the silhouette of a stag's head. We found a spot with a good view of the action and sat down on the grass.

One of the knights – silver dragon – was a good two inches taller than the other and seemed to have more finesse to his game, a fluidity to his movements as he swung and thrust at his foe. Ellis, sitting next to me, was in a trance of admiration.

Eventually, stag's head could take no more and was felled by silver dragon with a theatrical strike to the head. Ellis punched the air and joined in the applause as the victor took a sweeping bow.

Then, with a lumbering swagger I found all too familiar, he began to walk in our direction, removing his helmet as he did so. And that's when my worst suspicions were confirmed.

'Vince!' Ellis said, springing up from the grass and ducking under the rope, running towards him. Vince scooped him up in his arms and hoisted him into the air, and a few people in the crowd cooed with mawkish delight. It made me want to take Vince's sword and scythe them down like wheat stalks.

I hadn't set eyes on him since Kirsten's funeral. He'd sobbed convulsively through the whole thing — his pale slab of a face creased with grief — and you would have had to have been a heartless prick not to feel sorry for him. I wept, too, but it was for the mother my son had lost, not the former spouse with whom I had long fallen out of love, even if by the end we had been getting on better than we ever had.

I couldn't see him clawing his way out of that abyss of grief for years, had assumed he would shut out the world, maybe even drink himself to death on the fine single-malt whisky he loved.

Evidently this hadn't happened. This wasn't even Old Vince — the plump Christmas turkey in a parrot's plumage. This was New Vince. Lean — or at least lean*er* — bright-eyed, his Hell's Angel beard traded in for a goatee so neat it looked like the work of a surgeon's scalpel, not a razor. Layers of sorrow seemed to have been peeled off him like an onion. And was that a pair of gym-sculpted pectorals lurking beneath the swirling bas-relief of his bronze breastplate? Vince hadn't been hitting the bottle; he'd been hitting the bench-press.

'Nick!' he said, putting Ellis down and giving me an unexpected bear hug when previously a wary handshake was all we'd been able to muster. 'Thanks for coming — and for bringing this little guy.'

Ellis gazed up at him with a look that was, for me, a little too close to adulation for comfort.

'Cool sword!' Ellis said.

'Here, you can hold it if you like,' Vincent said, taking it out of its scabbard and handing it to Ellis, who held it in his upraised palms like a sacred relic.

'Wow! It's heavy.'

'Watch you don't cut yourself,' I said.

'It's fine, it's not sharp at all,' Vince said.

'So you couldn't have killed the other knight, even if you wanted to?' Ellis asked.

'Remember what I told you about those American wrestlers on the telly?' I said. 'It's all pretend.'

'Well, true, but like wrestling it requires tremendous skill,' Vince said, looking at Ellis. 'I did a swordsmanship course with a guy who trains Hollywood actors.'

'I'll give Russell Crowe a bell,' I said. 'You can be his stunt double for Gladiator 2.'

'How about I show you a few moves, champ?' he said to Ellis, ignoring my comment. 'That alright with you, Nick?'

'Knock yourself out,' I said.

I went to the food van to get some hotdogs and a couple of drinks, and as I stood in the queue, just a few metres away, I watched Ellis and Vincent, found myself mesmerised by their easy interaction. By the time I returned, they were sitting down on the grass chatting about fifteenth-century battle strategies.

'Shit, sorry, Vince, did you want anything?' I asked, handing Ellis a hotdog. 'Let me go back and get you a drink at least.'

'It's fine,' he said, getting up. 'Gotta get back to the action anyway. My next event starts in a minute. We'll catch up later.'

Vince disappeared into one of the marquees and Ellis and I tucked into our food, soaking up the atmosphere as pearls of sweat slid off our sunscreened faces. A family sitting on a picnic rug beside us — a mother and father with their two children — had caught Ellis' eye. A look of sadness passed across his face.

'You okay, kiddo?' I said, putting my hand on his shoulder. He nodded and smiled and I wiped a smear of tomato sauce off his face with my thumb. He leaned into me, his arm around my back, but Vince, to my dismay, wasn't there to see it.

After a while, he emerged from the marquee clad in some kind of padded suit and holding a wooden stick and shield. An MC, talking through a loud-speaker, announced something called the 'Spectator Challenge' and asked the audience for a brave volunteer to take on 'Vincent the Valiant'. A couple of tentative hands went up in the crowd and I found myself joining them — perhaps with a little more enthusiasm.

'We have a challenger,' the MC said, pointing me out and beckoning me into the roped enclosure.

'Er, are you sure about this, Dad?' Ellis said, as I wolfed down the last of my hotdog and got to my feet.

'It's just like wrestling, remember? A bit of fun. Just wait here and stay where I can see you.'

I walked over to the MC who asked me my name. 'Nick,' I said. 'Nick Hinton.'

'Lords and ladies,' he said, speaking into his microphone. 'I present to you, Noble Nick of Hintonshire.'

He gave me a bunch of padding that looked like the stuff a cricket player might wear — leg pads, helmet, gloves, as well as a contraption that fitted across the chest. Then, after he had helped me put it all on, he handed me a long wooden baton and a round shield. I was already saturated with sweat.

Vince came over as the MC helped tighten my helmet strap. 'What are you doing, Nick?' he said.

'You two know each other?' the MC said.

I said nothing, waited for Vince to respond but he just stood there looking at me, eyes narrowing. Eventually he raised his hand to the MC and said, 'It's okay, Clive, we're good here.'

The MC shrugged and ushered us into the centre of the enclosure. I swished my baton around a few times like a mad conductor, getting the feel of it, loosening myself up. I'd boxed throughout my youth and I was confident that my pugilistic background — sharp reflexes, calves like steel urns, even after all these years — would give me an advantage. I adopted a southpaw stance and the MC, stepping away, shouted, 'Let battle commence!'

I attempted a little Muhammad Ali foot-shuffle, a bit of showmanship for the audience, but the weight of the padding made me almost topple over. Then I advanced on Vince, who seemed startled by my offensive tactics.

My first thrust glanced off the edge of his shield and I almost lost my balance. Then he somehow managed to get around the side of me, jabbing me in the ribs with the tip of his baton. I went for a low blow around the top of his thighs where there was an inviting gap between the padding, but he sprang back with an agility I had to admit was impressive.

'Dirty fighter, eh?' he said. 'Well two can play at that game, mate.'

He feinted with his baton then barged into me with the shield, sending me staggering backwards, my arse eventually finding the rock-hard ground with a dull thud. Then he stood right over me, sword poised above his head, executioner-style.

I closed my eyes and prepared for both the coup de grace and the humiliating walk of shame in front of the crowd, all the way back to where Ellis was waiting for me. But Vince seemed to have frozen in mid-air.

'Oh for god's sake, Vince,' I said, opening my eyes and looking up at him. 'Don't milk it.'

'What were you trying to prove, Nick?' he said.

He turned to look at Ellis, who was now standing at the rope, as though ready to run over and intervene. There were murmurs of impatience among the crowd. Someone shouted 'No mercy!' and a few people jeered in accordance.

'Roll to your left,' Vincent said in an urgent whisper.

'What?'

'For god's sake, Nick. Just roll to your left. *Quickly*!'

I did as he said, and with two hands he brought the baton down with force, spearing it several inches into the turf beside me. Hunched over, he made a big show of trying to pull it out. As if, like Excalibur, it was embedded in stone. And as he did so I managed to clamber to my feet and perform a mock decapitation. Obligingly, Vince keeled over and lay splayed out on the grass, still as a corpse, and the crowd burst into applause.

'We have a winner!' the MC said, raising my arm aloft, although that was the last thing I felt like.

**

After removing my padding and cooling off a little, I took Ellis for a walk around the fairytale village — 'too babyish', he said — and the orangery. We had an hour to kill before we were due to meet up with Vince again. I felt he was owed a little one-on-one time with Ellis, especially after his act of clemency in battle.

We ended up in the castle courtyard cafe and I ordered a bowl of ice cream for Ellis and carrot batons and low-fat hummus for me. I was thinking it might be time I took a leaf out of Vince's book, enrol in a gym, shed some of that excess timber.

I wanted to be around a long time for my boy, be the best dad I could be, play football with him in the park without getting out of breath. I pictured us taking mountain hikes together, running marathons. Truth be told, I also wanted to be able to look down for the first time in years and see my own penis without the use of a mirror, maybe get back to a 32-inch waist and find myself a nice girlfriend.

'Can we try archery and watch the jousting next, Dad?' Ellis said, mashing his three different-flavoured scoops into one with his spoon.

'Jousting's your specialist subject, so Mrs Morgan tells me,' I said.

He laughed nervously, his cheeks reddening.

'And my fishing rod is bloody knackered. You can't go damaging other people's property, Ellis.'

'I know. Sorry, Dad.'

'It's okay. I've never been good with the discipline stuff, have I?'

He shrugged his shoulders.

'Your mum was better at it. Better at everything, really.'

'Not better at Lego.'

I laughed. 'Yeah, maybe I had the upper hand there.'

'Vince is rubbish at Lego, too.'

'Good at this medieval lark, though.'

'Pretty good.'

'He's alright, isn't he? Vince?'

'I thought you kind of hated him?'

'I don't hate anybody, Ellis. I just didn't really know him.'

'Okay, Dad,' he said, before his face was suddenly illuminated with a smile. A smile that, for now at least, comprised an uneven mix of milk and adult teeth, punctuated by one vacant vermillion socket in the bottom row, awaiting its new occupant.

'What's that smile for?'

'I knew the swordfight wasn't real,' he said. 'But it was

still pretty cool. Especially at the end when you rolled over and Vince missed you.'

'You liked the rolling over, did you?'

'It was the best bit.'

The family who had been sitting next to us on the grass earlier entered the cafe and sat at a table near the door. Ellis watched them. The girl was about his age, the boy a little younger.

'Ellis, if you could have stayed with Vince, after Mum died, would you?'

I knew it was no question for a seven-year-old and I immediately despised myself for asking it.

He squirmed in his seat and stared down at the table.

'Don't worry. There's no right or wrong answer. Whatever you say won't make any difference to anything.'

He slowly stirred his ice cream, the spoon gripped in his fist. 'He's not my dad.'

'That's not what I asked.'

'I don't have to go and live with Vince, do I?' he said, and I noticed the almost imperceptible shift in his features, the saline shine along the lower eyelids. 'Don't make me!'

'No, Ellis,' I said, reaching over and squeezing his hand. 'No, of course not.'

'Good. Because I want to stay with you forever.'

**

We tried the archery — Ellis got two bullseyes — watched the jousting and then we slowly made our way over to meet Vince at the field where they were giving children's pony rides. On the way, we passed the coat of arms stall, and this time I caved in to Ellis's request.

The woman showed us a list of basic templates and

images we could incorporate into our design. There were prancing stags, imperious-looking eagles, an assortment of mythological creatures — from griffins to unicorns — as well as swords, chalices and harps. The customer chose the elements and the woman blended them together on a laptop with her graphic-design wizardry, after which it would be printed out and framed.

Ellis settled on a shield flanked on one side by a bear — his choice; he said it reminded him of a stuffed toy his mother had once given him — and a dragon on the other, which I picked, ever the patriot.

'Can we hang on it my bedroom wall, Dad?' he said. 'Next to my Man United poster?'

'Sure, wherever you want.'

'And the banner?' the woman said. 'You can choose some words to go underneath. Maybe a motto. Or your initials, if you like.'

'D for Dad,' Ellis said, with gratifying certainty. 'And E for Ellis – that's me.'

'Is that it?' she said. 'Anything else?'

Ellis looked at me, then his eyes wandered over to the field where Vince was already standing, waving at us. He had changed into his civvies — baggy shorts and one of his lurid shirts. It may have been the one he wore when we had our handbags-at-dawn moment at the M4 service station. The episode seemed absurd now, and I sensed the time wasn't too far away when we could laugh at it together.

'Go ahead, Ellis,' I said. 'It's okay.'

But he needed me to say it, and I was fine with that.

'And a V, too,' I said to the woman. 'A V, an E and a D.'

Then I took my son's hand and we walked over to where Vince stood waiting for us.

A Cloud of Starlings

Philippa Holloway

She is almost home when she sees them, senses them first. It is dusk, the sun just gone below the stone wall of the top field, and she is easing the car between tight hedgerows when there is a faint crunch beneath the tyres, felt more than heard. She drops to a lower gear, slows and searches the road with tired eyes.

There are dark shapes, lumpen and irregular, scattered in the lane.

She stops, unease pooling in her gut, glances around at the darkening fields, grey sheep drifting beyond the wire fence and bare hawthorn branches, then back at the road as if the scattering might have vanished. But no, there are dead birds littering the lane, and if she drives on, she will crush them beneath the wheels of her car.

She is only a few hundred metres from home, can see the dark shape of their farmhouse on her right, the warm beacon of light from the kitchen window. Today was her day to work, a long shift at the hospital, paperwork piled on the passenger seat, and her husband is cooking dinner somewhere beyond these tiny wind-ruffled corpses. She wants the warmth of her hall to envelop her, the glass of wine he'll pour when he hears her car pull up, the embrace of her daughter like a fierce rugby tackle hitting her side before she even has time to slip off her shoes and stash them on the rack.

She wants routine.

She eases the car forward, trying to steer around the bodies, and feeling her failure through the tyres. As she reaches the apex of the curved lane, she stops again. There are too many. Hundreds, perhaps. The headlights pick out the branches of the raggedy hawthorn in sharp grey spikes and there are more birds caught there, suspended in the bare twigs, heads lolling. It's as if an entire flock has fallen from the sky.

She can't bear to drive over them, kills the engine instead and fills her arms with the files, her heavy bag tugging her shoulder. The wind flutters the pages in her arms, threatening to tear them loose and release them into the air, and her hair whips into her mouth, cuts her vision. She picks her way through the dead birds, careful not to tread on their wing tips or curled toes. A macabre hopscotch.

In the porch she struggles with her load, manages to turn the key in the lock and tumbles into the hallway. She can hear the radio on in the kitchen, but no child rushes for her waist, and no one calls out a greeting. She dumps the folders on the sideboard and walks through into the kitchen. Dan is leaning over the stove, sniffing the steam rising from a cassoulet pan.

'Where's Sophie?' she asks.

'Christ, Siân! You made me jump!' He replaces the lid and rests his hand on his chest, right where his heart is now racing. 'I didn't hear you get back.'

'I had to leave the car in the lane. Have you seen the birds?' She goes to the fridge, takes out a half-empty bottle of wine and pours a glass. It doesn't taste as good as last night, a sour aftertaste near the back of her tongue.

'Yeah, we found them on the way home from school.'

'And you didn't think to clear the path?'

'The police told us not to. They want to send someone round, find out what's going on.'

'You called the police?'

'Yeah, of course. You don't think it's weird?'

'Of course it's weird, but is it really a police matter?'

'Well, who else would you call?'

She thinks for a moment, unsure. Who do you call when birds start falling from the sky? She walks over to the back window, to where the sun has slipped behind the horizon and the floodlights from the nuclear power station are competing with the sunset. It isn't close, but close enough. A low, sandcastle-shaped block just over a mile away. No, if it were that there would have been alarms, evacuations.

'I have no idea,' she says, and takes a gulp of the wine. 'So, when can we clear the road?'

'Tomorrow sometime.'

Tomorrow it is his turn to work: twelve hours on the road in his green uniform, waiting in lay-bys for a heart attack or RTA to fill his time. Half the time he's bored, half the time so busy his shifts run over by four or seven hours at a stretch.

Siân wanders through to the lounge, sees Sophie hunched over the dining table. A skinny girl, just turned twelve. Small for her age and still in pigtails and baggy jeans. She walks over, expecting to see homework, but finds her adding to extensive notes in an A4 sketchbook, the opposite page filled with a detailed study of a bird's face and feather patterns. One word is bolder than the others, as if she's pressed too hard with the pencil. WHY?

'What are you doing, Sophs?'

'Research.' She doesn't look up, doesn't squeeze her eyes shut against her mother's chest as if she wished she were still small, carriable.

Siân stands behind her daughter, admiring the delicate tracing of the feather patterns, the perfectly proportioned head and beak.

'Did you copy it?'

'I took photos.' She swipes her finger across her phone and the screen is filled with the stark image of a dead bird, head lolling just as in the drawing, claws curled closed. Its chest is petrol green and speckled. A starling. Her daughter glances up, as if for approval, but with worry shimmering in a fine line beneath her eyes.

'It's a brilliant sketch, Sophs.'

Sophie almost replies, but is cut off.

'Dinner is nearly ready!' Dan's head peeking round the door. 'Time to pack up, okay? Siân, can you set the table?'

Sophie carefully closes the book, replaces her pencils in their tin one by one and in order of hardness: 2H, H, F, HB, B…

Despite the hearty stew ladled onto her plate, and the hours that have dragged since lunchtime, Siân's appetite is compromised. The chicken, so tender it slides off the bone, reminds her too much of the soft crush beneath her tyres. She picks at the carrots instead, spearing them from the stock with her fork.

'Good day at school?'

Sophie is quiet, similarly averse to eating her meat. She doesn't eat much anyway, so this isn't unusual. She shrugs, avoiding the question. Siân and Dan exchange a glance. She's struggling to make friends, despite the move to a better school, one that can support her needs. One without bullies, they hope.

'Did you have Science today?' Her favourite subject, that she hopes will lead to a medical career like her parents. She doesn't know yet, thinks Siân, what a brutal route that is.

'Why do you think they died, Mum?'

'Let's not talk about it at the dinner table, huh?'

'But…'

'Let's not.'

And yet none of them can think of anything else all evening.

'I've got a migraine.'

Sophie is still under the duvet, refusing to get up and dressed for school. Siân kneels beside the bed.

'I know it's difficult, sweetheart. I know. But you need to go in. The more you go, the easier it will be.'

'But my head hurts. My eyes hurt. My stomach is sick.'

Siân lays her hand on her child's forehead as if this might tell her what the matter is. Eleven years of training and specialising, and when it's her own daughter she resorts to a palm on the face. She's convinced the symptoms are fake, but not convinced enough to force her to get dressed, eat breakfast and then walk past the scene in the lane. If she stays home they can both avoid it, watch TV all day, pretend nothing is the matter.

'You're not faking?'

'I promise, Mummy. It hurts when I move my head.'

'Okay. I'll get painkillers, you stay there. No phone though, if your head is bad. It'll only make it worse.'

Sophie scowls, but knows she can't argue. Sian goes to the kitchen, her daughter's phone in one hand. She runs the tap for cold water and gets distracted by the searches her child has made on the smartphone's browser.

Murmuration.

Curse.

Radiation.

Meaning of dead birds.

Electromagnetic pulse.

How to dissect a bird.

Diseases in starlings.

The times are listed too: 11.58pm, 12.14am, the last one at 2.32am. No wonder she is tired and headachey. She takes the paracetamol tablets upstairs and watches her child swallow them easily, supresses a vague melancholy when the memory of sticky pink Calpol surfaces, a nostalgia for teething fevers and chickenpox and all those manageable traumas that can be soothed away with strawberry flavours and cuddles.

'Will you be okay if I go down and do some work?'

Sophie nods, eyelids heavy. The room is stuffy and hot. She'll be back to sleep soon, Siân thinks.

Two hours later, the kitchen is sparkling clean and there is paperwork covering the desk in Siân's study. She has almost forgotten her daughter, upstairs, sleeping, as she peer-reviews an article on how to manage parental expectations in cases of childhood brain tumours. She has read the line *many parents will struggle to align expectations of their child's pre-illness perceived futures with the reality of their new disabilities and needs* at least six times, stuck on a loop of self-reflection. What was she expecting when Sophie was born? She knows she tried hard not to imagine, not to build a picture of a fantasy family that might never fruit. They've been lucky, haven't they? Sophie has suffered none of the terrible physical illnesses she herself has seen decimate families before her eyes. But her daughter isn't what she expected, and now that thought has been released it can't be caught again.

A flash of movement catches her eye, through the window. A white van glimpsed through hedges as it navigates the lane. She is grateful for the distraction, despite dreading their arrival all morning. She lays the article carefully on the desk so she won't lose her place, and fetches her coat and wellies, ready to talk to the police, to face the carnage at the boundary of her garden.

It's sunny, clear and cold, and she keeps her hands in her pockets as she walks down the lane, standing at one end of the tideline of bodies while the van disperses three people, their ages and genders hidden by white hooded cover-alls and blue plastic booties, at the other side. She waves, calls a greeting that seems inappropriately cheerful under the circumstances, as if she is hailing the milkman or postman.

One of the people starts to navigate a path through towards her, like a spaceman walking on alien land; arms and legs thick puffy white, shapeless feet lifted unnaturally high, gait unnaturally slow. Siân shuffles her feet, begins to worry about her own attire. Are they wearing the forensic suits to protect the scene or themselves? She starts to walk towards them, as if meeting in the middle will somehow negate the threat, share out the unpleasantness between them, but the person in the suits holds up a hand, calls through their mask 'No, stay there. I'll come to you.'

When they arrive at her side the person pulls down their mask, smiles. A woman, taller than Siân and with soft crinkles around her eyes that immediately soothe.

'So, what the heck happened here?' she asks.

'I thought it was your job to tell us.'

'A joint effort, probably. Are you Siân Evans?'

Siân nods. The other two people are already photographing the scene, one kneeling for close-ups on the ground, the other taking a wide shot before focussing on the birds caught in the hedge spikes and wire fence. Siân turns briefly to glance at the house, catches sight of her daughter like a pale ghost in the window. Big round eyes that give her an alien visage. It takes Siân a moment to realise Sophie is using binoculars, studying the scene. It takes another few moments for her to realise she is secretly wishing her daughter was at school, playing video games, watching trash on TV like a normal pre-teen rather than obsessing over the birds in the lane. The thoughts crowd and split, disperse and settle somewhere out of sight as the woman starts asking questions.

'When did this happen, then?' She has a small digital voice-recorder in her outstretched hand.

'Don't you need my ID or something, first? To record our details?'

'Nope, it was all logged last night. You are Mrs Evans? This is your property?'

She has sowed the seeds of doubt, corrects it. 'Yes, sorry. And I don't know exactly. I was at work, didn't get home until...maybe ten to six? It was already dark, or almost dark.'

'Did anyone else see what happened?'

'Wasn't that logged last night?' She is trying to keep the edge off her voice, but is frustrated with the pace so far, wants to go back inside and get Sophie away from the window. 'Sorry. No, my husband found them when he got back from the school run, at about four o'clock. He'd been shopping beforehand, left the house at maybe two-ish? There was nothing there then.'

'Did he tell you if he saw anything unusual before he left? The birds moving oddly? Any strange smells? A predator, maybe?'

'What kind of predator?' Siân's heart leaps involuntarily, images of panthers or skulking teens with pellet guns lurking in the ditches or behind the old stone walls near the bottom field. Faceless and fearless.

'Birds of prey?'

'There's a pair of sparrowhawks that nest nearby. But how —'

'Hello!' The woman is looking past Siân, smiling.

Sophie is standing in the lane, jeans and wellies on under

64

her nightdress, her heavy winter coat open and flapping in the breeze.

'Sophs! Go back in!'

Sophie comes closer, unusually defiant. Stands right at the tideline of bodies, her face serious, a question dimpling her brow. She slips a skinny hand into Siân's and watches as the other two investigators start taking samples of soil and holding strips of reactive paper in the air before sealing them into plastic tubes.

'Not at school today?' The woman asks Sophie, pulling her hood back.

'I'm ill.'

'Ill?' This question directed at Siân, a hard undertone.

'I'd better get her back indoors, do you need anything else?'

'I'll follow you up in a minute, just to check what her symptoms are, if that's okay?'

'Of course, I'll put the kettle on.' She squeezes Sophie's hand perhaps a little too tightly as she leads her back to the house. The tech-induced headache will now be logged, taken into account. Evidence. She knows because she herself has picked out the tiniest clue in her patients' conversations, grasped at every route to causality and diagnosis so many times. She can't fault the investigator; just hopes she is being overcautious. Sophie is fine, nothing wrong with her at all.

In the sky between her and the sea a murmuration of starlings spins and dives, but Siân doesn't notice. She is too busy trying not to think.

By late afternoon the lane is clear. Siân couldn't wait until Dan got home, couldn't rely on him finishing on time or having the energy to sweep and bag the birds even if he did. She hoped the police would remove them, but when she asked they just shrugged and replied that they didn't have the facilities. They took just five bodies, each sealed in individual plastic bags and packed inside the kind of insulated container that is used to transport organs or picnics. Siân stood in the lane and watched them leave, fury building at the mess at her feet as the white van flashed in and out of sight between the hedgerows then vanished beyond the copse near the junction. She'd left it for a while, drinking tea in her study, trying to edit the rest of the paper. *Sometimes the death of an afflicted child is a relief for parents of multiple children, as it signals a return to a familial routine more culturally accepted as normative. For those with only one child, however, it can trigger feelings of failure and remorse, during which the expectations of normative life from before diagnosis are reignited…*

When she did go out, with a garden broom and shovel, a wheelbarrow, she covered her mouth with a scarf and wore thick gardening gloves. Hardened herself to the smear and scrape as she heaped the birds and wheeled them down to the boundary ditch. She piled them high, tossed in dry logs from the stack that feeds their log burner, and stood back while the pyre burned. Smoke twisting and swirling, dark against the clear winter sky. Once the fire was dampened, she stripped in the kitchen, shoved her clothes in the washing machine and spent over half an hour beneath the hot spray of the shower, washing her hair three times to get the smell of smoke and burnt feathers out.

She knows she should go back to her study, finish the paper and close the file before dinner. But she remembers her promise, her first plan – afternoon TV, chocolate treats, cuddles – an easy way for them to forget the trauma of the night before and this morning. Dan might be home in time for a late supper. She can do Sophie a pizza, send her to bed early and then cook something special. Open a fresh bottle. Back to routine.

She turns on the TV in the lounge and goes to look for her daughter, expecting to find her in her bedroom with a book, or drawing something detailed and far too advanced for her age in one of her sketchbooks, but her room is empty. She walks through the house calling, checks the bedrooms and kitchen, checks the lounge again in case Sophie was in there, curled in a corner somewhere and so quiet maybe Siân missed her when she drifted through earlier. She is just beginning to panic, her mind in a contiguous state of denial and worry, when she thinks to check the garden.

Out the back there is a large covered porch, sheltered from the wind by glazed panels, a view across the fields and towards the coast. The nuclear power station hunkers half-hidden behind tall conifers on the edge of the view. Sophie is there, the table where they eat summer suppers covered with newspaper sheets, three dead birds laid out in a row. She is wearing Perspex goggles from an old toy chemistry set, blue nitrile gloves and a plastic apron almost certainly taken from Siân's study or Dan's paramedic bag. She is holding a small paring knife, the sharpest knife in the house, and just as Siân steps onto the decking makes a clean incision down the breast of the first bird.

Siân bites her tongue, doesn't want to cry out or shout in case her daughter's hand – small and skinny inside those baggy blue gloves – slips and slices her own flesh open. She stands mesmerised as the child uses her thumbs to prise open the chest wall of the bird, muttering something under her breath. An incantation or self-reassurance, Siân can't quite tell. Either way it raises the hairs on her arms and makes her stomach pool to liquid. This is an unnatural juxtaposition of work and home, her daughter the fulcrum of the uncanny balance. Sophie pauses, peering inside the thorax, then checks the information on the iPad next to her.

67

If she closes her eyes, takes only the outline of her child into her head, Siân can imagine her daughter is painting, or crafting something innocent and colourful out of Play-Doh or clay. Can sink into the pastel-coloured memories of the expectations she carried along with the bump of her pregnancy. But when she opens them again her daughter is pulling out the entrails of a dead starling. Siân watches as she begins removing organs, sealing them in small plastic food bags and weighing them on the digital kitchen scales, noting down the details in her sketchbook. She is fascinated by her child's apparent calm: this child who cried for a month when they hit a hare on the road to Abersoch one balmy summer's evening, who can't watch adverts appealing for animal charities, or throw away a stuffed toy. This child who struggles to make friends, to make eye contact, to walk without tripping, is suddenly an elegant surgeon, half-woman, precise.

Siân shuffles onto the porch, letting her presence be known. Bites back her instinct to gather the corpses into the newspaper and throw them out. Instead, she moves and sits opposite, waits for Sophie to speak.

'Are you mad at me?' The gloved hand shaking slightly, the knife poised over the emptied torso.

'No, baby. But what are you doing?'

'An autopsy.'

'Why?'

'Because I need to know.' Her eyes are wide behind the goggles, her shoulders tight. 'Will you help me?'

Siân pauses, for no more than a second or two, but it's enough for disappointment to cloud Sophie's eyes. She looks down at the dead bird, tears welling.

'No. I think you're doing a perfectly good job yourself. But I'll sit with you and answer any questions you may have.'

The eyes flash back up, a half-smile flickering. 'Really?'

'Of course. Now, what have you found so far?'

'Everything inside is normal. And the wing-patterns aren't messed up, like the ones after the Sher…Chor…'

'Chernobyl disaster?'

'Yes.'

Neither of them glance out of the window. Siân tries not to let the molten burn of self-criticism show in her face. How does her daughter know these things? There are filters on their internet settings: no violence, no porn. She always expected those two to be the biggest threat. But science and history contain both, she realises. What has her daughter read? How many times has Siân let her down?

'Anything else?'

'There is blood on their nostrils, every one. And their necks are really floppy, but I don't know if it's just because they are dead or if they are broken.'

Siân slips on a spare pair of gloves and carefully feels down the spine of a bird, from its eggshell thin skull to its delicately ridged hips, returns to the neck and locates the fault.

'Let me feel that one.'

Sophie hands over another bird, and Siân finds the same fault, in a similar place. She considers lying, feigning ignorance, but can't decide what benefit there would be. Would not knowing that both birds have broken necks actually help her daughter any more than finding out the truth?

'Well?'

'Here,' Siân hands one bird back and guides her daughter's sheathed hands into place, talks her through the exam. Watches as her daughter finds the loose connection in the bird's beaded spine. A smile of triumph, a frown of thought.

'Both of them?'

Siân nods.

'All of them?'

Siân shrugs. 'Maybe. We'll have to wait and see what the experts think.'

Sophie nods, satisfied for now, and together they clear the table, wrapping each bird carefully in newspaper and laying them on the back step while they wash the knife and scales, disinfect the table. Before they remove and dispose of the gloves and apron, they bury the birds in a shallow grave in the neglected flower border, and Sophie marks the spot with a smooth, rain-polished stone. As they finish a huge murmuration of starlings rises into the sky a few fields away, twisting like smoke, darkening with density and then dispersing. They watch for a while, entranced, disturbed, and Sophie's hand creeps into Siân's, clings tight.

'I used to think that was beautiful,' she whispers, 'but now I just think it's frightening. Like they're going to turn and swoop down on me.'

Siân squeezes back.

'They'd never do that. They're just flying, having fun or hunting flies. Let's go and eat chocolate and watch TV, hey?' And they turn their backs on the birds and go into the creamy warmth of the lounge, where they both pretend to enjoy the film despite neither of them caring at all what happens.

A week later the phone rings. Sophie is in the bath, Dan cooking, so Siân answers.

'Mrs Evans?'

'Speaking.'

'It's Sally Winters, from the forensic team? We came out last week to investigate the sudden death of a flock of birds on your property?'

'Yes.' Siân's heartrate picks up a notch, fearing a bad toxicology report, news of a radiation leak, warnings about new predators in the area.

'Well, our investigations have found nothing suspect or worrying at all, it seems the birds died from blunt force trauma, and considering the scale of the incident we conclude this was caused by them flying into the ground at speed.'

'Flying into the ground? Why would they do that?'

'We can't know for sure, but occasionally birds in large flocks get confused—'

'Confused? Birds don't just get confused and fly into the floor!' Her voice is rising, and she checks it, tries to hush in case Sophie hears.

'I understand your concern Mrs Evans, but there have been previous cases, not in the UK, but elsewhere, that have shown that, very rarely, when startled by something like a hawk or predatory bird and trying to perform evasive manoeuvres, they fail to pull up in time and fatalities can occur. These birds were distracted, travelling too fast. They made a mistake.'

But nature doesn't make mistakes like that, surely? Siân thinks. It's humans who miscalculate, who slip up, who say the wrong thing in a consultation with the parents or push the scalpel in a fraction of a millimetre too far… nature is far more carefully programmed, instincts honed and in tune with the rest of the planet. Birds don't fly into things because they aren't using their judgement, they are just… flying.

'Are you still there, Mrs Evans?'

'Yes, thank you for letting me know… I'm relieved it's not…'

'No problem, take care.'

And the line clicks dead.

Sophie is calling for help, for someone to hold the showerhead over her while she rinses the conditioner out of her long hair. Siân takes the stairs slowly, words from the article coming back to her mind in flits and starts: *Practitioners must be aware that parents of terminally ill children will always seek answers, even when there are none to give…*

'Who was it, Mum?' Sophie's skin is deep pink where the hot water has caused the blood to rush to the surface. She sits with one arm folded around her knees, her budding chest covered. She is twirling a wet lock of dark hair around her finger, studying the split ends. She hates hairdressers, can't abide the tickle and tug of a cut.

'It was the police, calling about the birds.'

The finger stops, her attention caught. She waits, not quite breathless.

'It was an accident. They said the birds just flew into the ground.'

Sophie pauses to think it over.

'No. Tell me what really happened.'

'That's what happened, Sophie. And if you think about it, that's what our findings indicated too.'

'But birds can't just fly at the floor, they'd move!'

They may even seek to blame medical personnel on whom they have placed unrealistic and/or unpredicted expectations of power. While they might know the situation is beyond the control of medical staff, they may still harbour fantasies that their child will be 'the miracle' among the masses.

'They made a mistake, baby.'

'No, there must be a better reason, a real reason. Like magnetism, or a seismic tremor too low for us to detect.' Sophie's voice is thin in the steam from the bath. Desperate.

'Sometimes there isn't an answer Sophie, sometimes nature just… makes mistakes.'

Sophie looks at the taps, at her own distorted reflection.

'Like me?' she whispers.

'What do you mean?' But Siân already knows. Sophie is quite old enough to notice she isn't like the other children at her school, or the last school.

'Freaks, like me?'

Siân kneels and lifts the shower head off its cradle at the edge of the bath, runs the water until it's warm.

'You're not a freak, Sophs. You're just… special.'

'Special, as in "wrong". As in "weird". As in "don't be her friend, it might be catching".' Her face is buried in her knees. Siân has no idea what to say, never had any trouble at school herself. Always thought that Sophie would be the same as her, in miniature, with maybe Dan's nose or eyes, or sense of humour… but that she'd be recognisable in more than just her shape and form. Her daughter is a wet, lanky ball of tears. Lonely, unsure, and all Siân can do for a minute is hold the spray of water over her head and smooth the creamy conditioner out until the hair squeaks as she rubs her hand through it.

She stands and fetches a towel off the rail, wraps it around her child, and pulls her in tight for a hug.

If there is too much of a gap between expectations and reality, and parents struggle to adjust in time, there may need to be a referral to professional services for counselling and/or family therapy.

Siân takes her daughter's shoulders and stares her straight in her eyes, remembering the calm hand with the paring knife, the determined face beneath the goggles. She sees the woman her daughter could become.

'Special as in "smarter", as in "better than I ever hoped".'

Sophie holds her gaze, but Siân never wavers. In the field behind the house a murmuration of starlings lifts up, swirls, and settles, quiet for now.

Juice

Rosie Manning

Dominic thumps his forehead against the front door, then takes a step back and kicks it, leaving a black smear across the PVC. He winces. His feet already burn from slapping concrete for fifteen minutes in thin, rubber soles. Sweat stings the corners of his eyes and soaks through his shirt. Saliva thickens his throat. Squash, he just wants a pint of squash and to put his head in the fridge. Is that too much to sodding ask? He checks his trousers and the front pocket of his bag again. If Reggie had still been alive, he could have nipped next door and got the spare, but the Marchants have moved in and his mum hasn't given them one yet. Just as well, even the thought of having to face Owen Marchant – the zygomatically blessed, stacked fly-half, dime of the upper sixth – in his current minging state would be enough to break him.

A steady chain of traffic passes the front gate, clogging the stagnant air with dust and fumes. He coughs and a headache whacks him behind the eyes. September shouldn't be this hot. If it had been raining, like it usually bloody did in Pembs, he'd have stayed in the library and got his dad to pick him up on the way home. He should have known they'd be waiting. Three days in and he's already dealing with this shit. Stupid to think sixth form would be any different. Maybe he won't bother tomorrow, sack it off and go into town.

He walks around the side of the house, wrestling with an

overgrown buddleia to reach the gate. After a couple of squeaky wiggles to loosen the bolt, he's through to the garden. He dumps his bag by the kitchen door – locked – and wanders down to the old trampoline in the corner of the lawn. Becky's daily sun pilgrimage has worn a path, like a parting, through the bleached and brittle grass. Her towels are still out. Their tropical patterns, though faded and worn, are the only hint of colour in the garden. She'd flipped out when Owen moved in; bought herself a bunch of new undies for the washing line, and lay on the trampoline for hours, sucking in her stomach and pretending not to pay any attention to next door's upstairs windows.

Owen Marchant had the whole of Haverfordwest to move to, but no, it had to be here. Because that's what Dominic really needs right now, a permanent reminder of his own inferiority, right next door. He climbs onto the trampoline, the disc bobbing under his weight, and lies down. The smell of coconut tanning oil drifts up and mingles with his own sourness. He tries filling his mind with the swarm and buzz of a nearby strimmer, but a lump keeps rising in his throat. There's no point; he should just get it over with.

He takes his phone from his pocket. Opens Tik Tok. Scrolls for a few seconds. There it is. His stomach clenches as he watches the fifteen-second clip of Dylan tackling him to the floor and riding him like a rodeo horse as he struggled to get up. They'd carried on filming as he hurtled down the hill, arms and legs flailing, their laughter masked by some stupid piss-take of a song. Sitting up, he shields the screen from the sun. Twenty-seven comments, thirty shares, one hundred and two likes. Humiliation blisters his skin. He shoves his phone back in his pocket to stop himself from flinging it away. There's nothing he can do. It's spinning around the internet, at the mercy of the attention algorithms. His head throbs, sending pulses through his whole body. Winding a towel around his fist, he bites down on it as hard as he can. The scratchy cotton dries his mouth and makes him gag. Eyes watering, he extracts his hand and stares up at the back of the house. His bedroom window is open.

Next to the high wall that separates his house from the Marchants', there's a stack of breeze blocks. They're still there from when his dad built the kitchen extension two years ago. If he can get onto the roof, he can crawl up to his room. The blocks wobble as he stands on them. He reaches up and grips a stone that bulges out from the wall, just above his head. The cement scratches his fingertips. He finds a smaller lump with his foot, but his school shoes slip and he scrapes his chest against the stone. Cursing, he jumps down and removes his shoes and socks. He tries again. This time, his toes cling to the wall. He pulls himself, like a stick insect, high enough for his upper body to clear the guttering, then twists and throws himself onto the extension roof. For a panicky moment, he dangles, before swinging his leg up and climbing onto the tiles.

He sits, side-on to the wall, panting and rubbing his battered chest. The grazes sting. His nerves are still jittery after his run-in with Dylan and now his muscles, pathetic as they are, tremble with the extra adrenalin. Owen probably could have vaulted up in one. He glances down into their garden – ugh, even that could have fallen from a glossy magazine. They only moved in at the start of the holidays; yet Reggie's scrubby old back yard now has decking, veggie beds and bad-Hawaiian-shirt flowers. The old apple tree, laden with fruit, stands by a brand-new potting shed. Typical. It's all so bloody, sickeningly, perfect. A sprinkler shushes over the lawn, flinging out droplets. He sympathises with his own parched, post-apocalyptic-looking garden, longing for a rogue arc that might send a few drops its way. He's gagging for a drink.

He begins his crawl up towards his room. Lichen and clumps of moss crumble under his hands and knees. Above and to the right of him, from next door's upstairs window, something flashes. The sound of heavy bass starts up; the tinny melody muffled behind the glass. Another flash. A figure wearing gold is glinting and sparkling in the afternoon sunlight. They're dancing. Dominic flattens himself onto his stomach. Owen's an only child, maybe it's his mum? He feels his cheeks redden, but stretches his neck a bit higher. The figure comes to the window, props a little mirror on the sill, and bends forward to look into it. Dominic frowns, a twist of recognition – those cheekbones – but his brain takes a moment to catch up. Owen!

He looks different. His features are sharper, more defined. His eyes are wider, darker. His fluffy blonde hair is slick against his head. He's wearing a gold sequinned top. Automatically, Dominic reaches for his phone and swipes to video. He zooms in. The window is far enough away that the picture turns grainy. He raises his hand, trying to keep it steady. Owen is rooting around in a small bag. He pulls out a pen and twists it, presses the pen to his top lip, and in one deft movement, sweeps two scarlet arcs out from the centre and one across his bottom lip.

Dominic can't pull his eyes away. He lies rigid against the roof. Owen picks up the mirror and studies himself. As he lowers it, he glances up; Dominic whips his phone down. The movement catches Owen's eye. He leans forward and looks directly down at Dominic. They both freeze. Their eyes lock. Owen's breath mists the glass, Dominic's heart punches the roof tiles. Then, Owen pulls the curtain in front of him and the music abruptly stops. A blackbird, perching on the TV aerial, launches into song as Dominic scuttles up the roof to his room.

**

Early evening, Dominic lies bare chested on the living room floor, trying to focus on his Physics homework. The air in the room is muggy and stale, as if the carpet, sofa and armchairs are all breathing out at once. The house vibrates around him; the shower's overhead hum, the washing machine, Becky yakking on the phone in her room, Dad drilling god knows what in the Utility. He gives up, rolls onto his back, and plays the video of Owen on his phone for the tenth time.

It's unbelievable. He still can't get his head around it. What does it mean? Of course, he knows what it looks like, but what the actual fuck? This boy's life is charmed, he does whatever he wants, whenever he wants and everybody loves him. What is it, an act? Dominic can't even breathe without someone throwing shade. He just wants to be left alone, to be himself, with his books, his experiments, his quiet and unquiet thoughts, and all the raging confusions that have overtaken his body in the last year. And nobody will let him. Every fucking day is torment and Owen's swanning around with this hidden away. It isn't fair; he should know what it's like. He should be made to feel it too. He taps open Facebook.

The doorbell rings. Dominic jumps up, fumbling and dropping his phone. He'd nearly done it; posted it online for everyone to see. Heat rushes through him, sending his head spinning, like the time he'd set his bedroom carpet on fire with a blow torch, just smothering it before it reached the curtains. The bell rings again and he blinks. He grabs his T-shirt and pulls it over his head as he goes to answer the door.

On the doorstep stands Owen, toes almost touching the

threshold. He's holding a plastic bag. Dominic has to stop himself from leaping back. He opens the door wider and grips the handle. He's flushing and the awareness of it turns his face into a furnace.

'Hi,' says Owen. His hair is damp and ruffled in a clump on top of his head. His skin looks scrubbed and smooth, a hint of pink under the tan. The smell of mint hangs in the air between them.

'Hi.' The word sticks in Dominic's throat. He coughs; looks at the floor.

'I'm Owen.'

'Um, yeah, I know.' He nods.

'Oh. You do?' Owen frowns, tips his head to the side. 'You're—'

Dominic tells him before it can become a question.

'Yeah, Dominic, of course...'

Owen leans against the door frame, clamps his hands underneath his armpits and his biceps bulge forwards. He rests one flip-flopped foot on the lip of the doorway. His legs are completely hairless, but that's a rugby thing, right? Dominic feels like he's tipping sideways, he's never stood this close to him before. They're the same height, despite the twenty-month age gap. Owen will be eighteen in a few weeks. Dominic remembers him being cake-bombed outside the common room last year. Twenty months. Maybe that's all it will take for his scarecrow body to bulk out, to flatten the red raw mountain ranges erupting across his jaw, to pull the bits of himself together.

'I brought you these.' Owen holds out the bag, focussing on a spot just over Dominic's shoulder. Dominic takes it and peers inside. Owen moves back off the doorstep and puts his hands in the pockets of his shorts.

'Apples?'

'They're from our tree.'

'Right, er, thanks.' Dominic stares at the apples; pale green, pink-tinged, leaves and stalks still attached. He can't look up; flashes of sequins, lipstick, loop through his mind.

'So. Can you tell it's me?'

He nearly pukes. 'Uh, what? Tell what's you?'

Owen smiles, close-lipped and shakes his head. He exhales, looking briefly up into the porch. 'Look—'

Behind him, Dominic hears a thudding. He turns to see his mum coming down the stairs, her hair wrapped in a purple towel.

'Dom, who is it? Oh hi!' She's brought her shower scent with her too, something lemony. He feels rank and sticky between them. He moves aside to give her more room and she fills the doorway.

'Owen, right? I've been meaning to pop over, introduce ourselves to your mum and dad. How're you all settling in?'

'Yeah, all good, thanks.' Owen scuffs his flip-flops on the tiles.

'You're in STP too, aren't you?'

'Uh huh. Just started upper sixth.'

'Oh fab. Not long to go then?'

Owen catches Dominic's eye and stares, his jaw tightens. 'No. Just one more year to get through.'

Dominic shifts against the door and holds his breath.

'Oh, you boys. I'm sure it's not that bad. What you got planned for after? How'd the trial go with the Scarlets? Mark, Dom's dad, works with your cousin Paul. You're a legend in the making, I hear.'

'Er, no, I mean yeah, it was okay. I went to a couple of training sessions with them.' His cheeks are blotching pink. 'Dad wants me to sign up, but I'm not sure yet. I was thinking maybe London.'

'Ah love.' His mother gushes. 'You just gotta do what makes you happy, eh?'

'Er, yeah, guess so. Thanks.'

Dominic is cringing so hard he longs to shrivel into himself and disappear. The pause threatens to turn into a silence. He shoves the bag at his mum.

'Owen brought us some apples.'

'Ah lush, that's really kind. I've always loved that tree. Reggie used to be a bit of a miser with the fruit, bless him. He'd lob one or two over the wall occasionally.' She chuckles and takes the bag from Dominic.

Owen shrugs. 'We've got loads.' He pauses, turns to go. 'I guess I'll see you at school?'

'Uh yeah, sure.'

'It was lovely to meet you, thanks so much for the Scrumptious Discoveries.'

Owen stops and turns back, frowning. 'The – the what?'

'The apples.' His mum chuckles again. 'They're called Scrumptious Discovery. Daft, isn't it? Especially for a man as grumpy as Reggie.'

Owen blinks, his mouth twitches. He looks at Dominic and then explodes into laughter, great big snorting breaths of laughter. Dominic is transfixed as Owen struggles to control himself. Slowly, he realises that he is smiling too. A massive grin has spread across his face without him noticing. Like when he pretends not to be interested in his sister's rom-coms. His mother smirks at them.

'Er, right…see you then.' She leaves them to it, pulling the towel from her head and rubbing her hair.

Owen wipes the corner of one eye and draws in a deep breath.

'I'll see you…Okay?'

'Okay.'

Owen hesitates, opens his mouth as if to speak but only nods. He turns and walks through the front gate, letting it clang behind him. Dominic stays in the open doorway. The evening light is beginning to fade, the air warm and soft. An elderly man, shirtsleeves rolled up, shuffles along the pavement with his tiny dog. He raises his hand to Dominic, who raises his in return. Maybe he will go to school tomorrow after all.

**

Owen slugs the last of his coffee and walks through a gate in the school's perimeter fence. It's his third of the morning and his guts aren't thanking him for it. Chucking his cup in a bin, he checks his social media accounts – still nothing. He walks the tarmac path, eyes on the floor, towards the sixth form block. He's barely slept. Waking every couple of hours with a jolt, grabbing his phone, scrolling refreshing scrolling refreshing. What if he's got it wrong? Dominic seems alright, but he barely knows him. He can't be sure. Mad, starey eyes on him too, all kinds of browns and greens, but you couldn't say exactly which. Pretty freaky, especially when they've seen a part of your fucking soul. He groans to himself. Why did he have to use his phone? And those bloody apples; honestly you couldn't make this shit up.

At the common room door, he tenses his abs, then yanks it open. From the top of the stairs, he scans the room; Dewi by the vendors at the far wall, Matt and Lucy eating each other on that rancid sofa, miscellaneous goths in the corner, that messed-up prick Dylan and his idiots sitting on the tables, gurning over their phones. So far, so normal. No-one seems to be staring at him more than usual, except his stalker Gwennie, but he's used to that. He can't see Dominic anywhere. The common room appears to have a giant, gaping space right in the middle of it. He's never noticed that before. He scoots down the stairs and over to Dewi, as if expecting sniper fire.

'Alright O?'

'How's it going?'

'Yeah good, man. You training later?' Dewi pulls the foil from the protein shake he's got out of the vendor and takes a gulp.

'Like I got a choice, Mason would bloody cane me if I missed first session.'

'Ha, and he'd love it, the ol' perv.'

Owen ignores him. 'You seen that Dominic this morning?'

'Who?'

'Ne'mind, I'll go have a scout for him, he's got something of mine. Catch you later.'

He leaves through the door to the yard – probably best not to hang around in one place too much today. A patch of wall is slowly heating up in the morning sun. He leans against it and tries to decide at which entrance to catch Dominic. From the far end of the yard, a tall, hunched over figure is walking towards him. Head down, dark hair flopping over his face, hands low in his pockets. Owen moves to intercept him. Blank, multi-paned windows overlook him on either side. The rest of the concrete is in deep shade and he shivers as he crosses into the chill.

Halfway, he waits in the undercover space beneath the Geography corridor. Dropping his bag by a cylindrical pillar, he watches Dominic approach. He feels out of position, not used to being at the mercy of someone else's game plan. On the field, he makes the decisions. He can run the advantage and try and intimidate; force a mistake – it wouldn't take much to get Dominic flustered. Maybe he'll throw a dummy

83

pass or bring someone else into the line – he can say it was a dare, he'd had a bet with the other lads. Or, a kick to create more space – play the confessional, the confused sexuality card. He isn't confused, he knows exactly who he is, but he senses that Dominic is fighting his own battles on that front, and that's what matters.

'Hey.' Dominic's voice is quiet. He flicks his hair out of his face and meets him with a steadier gaze than yesterday. Something twinges, low down in Owen's stomach.

'Hiya. Alright?'

Dominic nods. 'Uh huh. You?'

He pauses before he answers; he's tired, so very, very tired. Fuck it. 'No, Dominic, funnily enough, I'm not. Kinda wondering what the play is, y'know? You gonna put me out of my misery?'

Dominic puffs out his cheeks, his eyes search Owen's face, his torso, down to his unlaced Dr Marten's. But he says nothing.

'Photo or video, at least tell me that?'

'Video,' Dominic mumbles.

'You little bitch,' he says, softly. 'You couldn't just sip tea, no?'

'It just…sort of happened. I wasn't thinking.' Dominic flinches as the morning bell rings, reverberating around them.

'Oh? Gossip radar just kicked in, did it? You haven't deleted it though, have you?' Owen steps closer to him. Dominic's mouth falls open slightly and his breathing sounds laboured. 'How many times you watched it?'

For a second he looks terrified, but Owen smiles and Dominic's shoulders visibly drop. The boy is clearly out of his depth, he has no idea what to do with any of this. There's a small, unlocking sensation in Owen's chest, a hint of release. Maybe it isn't so bad that he knows, maybe they could talk?

Around them the buildings are coming alive with the sound of hundreds of feet. Chattering voices pour through doors as kids cross the yard to the PE block. The noise swells, but Dominic seems oblivious to it; what does he want, where do they go from here?

Before Owen can think of something else to say, a body collides with Dominic, sending him staggering to one side. An arm swings around the back of his neck, pulling him down. He has to bend at the waist to get out of the grip. His school bag shunts up over his shoulders and falls onto the floor. Someone kicks it away from him. Dominic straightens up, eyes wide and darting about at the five figures encircling him. Owen curses, picks up his bag and moves away from them.

'Got yourself another beg-friend, Marchant? Another little groupie to follow you around?' Dylan's voice echoes through the underpass. 'What you got to talk about with ol' pretty boy here, Dommie? Showing him that little Tik Tok of mine, was you? How you like to get ridden good and proper.' He lunges at Dominic, reaching upwards to deliver two light taps to his cheek. Dominic jerks his head away. The other boys laugh like they're rattling cages.

Dylan juts his chin at Owen. 'Why you hanging about? Haven't you got a forward to go grease up or something?'

They are all looking at him now. Even Dominic, who has folded in on himself as if wearing a straitjacket. He wanders over to Dominic's bag, picks it up and skids it along the concrete towards him. He stays quiet. Dominic is still staring. Then something seems to close down in him and his face hardens. Slowly, his hand moves to his trouser pocket. His phone is half poking out.

'Hey boys.' Dylan nods his head at his mates. That idiot can smell fresh blood a mile off. 'I think we might have interrupted—'

Owen spits on the floor. 'Jesus Christ Dylan, do you have to be such a fucking throwback all the goddam time?'

Dylan bares his teeth. He thumps Dominic out of the way as he barges past him. Owen folds his arms across his chest. Dylan's a head shorter than him, but he's still a unit.

'The fuck you say?'

'Was it a first or second year you were harassing yesterday, up on the fields? Wanting her to get her tits out, you sick fuck.'

Dylan curls his lip. Owen uncrosses his arms and squares up to him. The other boys look uneasily at each other. They won't want a scrap with the whole rugby team. He leans forward. Dylan stinks of cigarettes and his breath is sweet with energy drink. But he's the first to break eye contact, turning back to Dominic, whose face has gone the colour of dinner-hall spuds. For a minute, they're all still. Two smaller lads run past them, yelling at each other. The smacks of their feet twang off the pipes in the wall. Dylan pulls a pouch of tobacco from his pocket and builds a rollie. He looks from Dominic to Owen and back again, nodding his head, then puts the rollie behind his ear and makes a sucking sound behind his teeth. He turns and walks away, backwards, watching them until the other boys follow and crowd in on him.

Whatever had begun to creep open inside Owen slams shut again. 'So that's how it's gonna be, is it?' He tries to keep his voice calm. 'Jerking me around like your own personal bodyguard?'

Dominic's eyes are wet, his jaw solid, barely moving to let the words out.

'I just want them to leave me alone.'

'Then grow a bloody spine!' It's out before he can stop it. Dominic is shaking, like the words are stacking up behind him.

'What, like you, you mean? Or a full, fucking exoskeleton in your case?'

The breath goes out of Owen. Pinned, he forces out a response.

'If that's what it takes to survive this dump.'

'Bullshit, that's such bullshit.'

'Oh?'

'You're scared, scared of being yourself.'

Owen gives a grim laugh. 'Right, how's that working out for you, mate? And, what exactly is myself – huh? You an expert in me all of a sudden?'

'No, I just—'

'You just what, got a glimpse and now think it's your fucking right to decide my story? I'm a lot of things, Dominic, like you I expect, but most people only want a simple version.'

'Well, I don't! And how the fuck can you know that if you never give anyone the choice?'

Owen's guts are jumping, he has a sudden urge to take a shit, or throw up. Just to let everything fall out of him, let it all go. He rubs his hands over his face, half expecting the skin to come away in sheets. He needs to move.

'Look,' he says, quietly. 'I could beat the crap out of you right now, if I wanted to, and I'd have no more problem. But lucky for you, I'm not Dylan. I'm training last lesson, till four. You come up the field and wait for me, I'll give you a lift home. You tell me then that you've deleted it, okay?'

He walks away, praying his legs don't give out on him.

**

The library is peaceful. Dominic closes his book. He leans over, resting his elbows on his knees, and places his cheek on the table's cool surface. A couple of girls chat quietly on the bean bags behind him. The book scanner beeps occasionally. The printer whirs to life, delivering someone's work. He's been in a trance all day, drifting through his lessons in overheated classrooms, ending up here for last period. His body is on automatic, his mind roams over Owen and what to do.

Something has rooted itself, something that wants to grow. Persistent shoots spreading towards the light, feathering his heart, expanding his lungs. Now it's started he doesn't know how to stop it. Doesn't know if he wants to stop it. What if Owen stops it, shunning him once he's deleted the video? He sits up. From the third floor, the library windows look down over farmland behind the school. A line of cloud is thickening, unrolling its shadow along the stubbled fields.

The last bell rings. He picks up his pencil case and the books that are sprawled in front of him, sliding them into his bag and closing the zip. He stands, puts his chair under the table and heads for the door, giving Mrs Lloyd a nod on his way out. Through the corridors, kids emerge in clumps from classroom doorways. He's conscious of their uniformed bodies as they jostle around him. Each bump and nudge from an elbow, or shoulder, confirms his solidity. His body is a boundary. He is contained. How can any of them possibly know what it's like to be him? And how can he know what it's like to be them? All the different homes they will go to, the things they will do, the people they will see.

He climbs the stairs to the main entrance; the heavy double doors have been wedged open to aid the evacuation. Outside the school, buses line up, like rumbling caterpillars awaiting their fill of little aphids. He walks behind one of them, getting a lungful of hot exhaust, as he crosses the road to the playing fields. Overhead, the clouds are darkening, bringing the sky lower and closer than the endless blue of the last six weeks. There's a pressure behind his eyes, across the bridge of his nose, in the hollows of his cheeks. He waits under a tree at the edge of the field, a few metres from the touch line. The ground is hard, the divots of mud and grass unyielding underfoot.

The squad are spread out. In the far corner, a group of eight are doing one-on-one scrummage drills. Two at a time, the boys stand facing each other, in a squat position, hands hovering over each shoulder. They touch, briefly, put their heads to the left, then engage. Pushing carefully against each other's bodyweight. Further up the pitch, to his left, the taller boys are in pods of four; two lifters, a jumper and a thrower. They take it in turns to launch each other into the air to catch the ball, as the thrower torpedoes it towards them. Six others are jogging laps, varying their speed at intervals, from a sprint to a stroll.

In the middle of the field is Owen. He is alone, kicking the ball high into the sky. He keeps his eyes on its trajectory, runs towards its landing point, and leaps. His arms extend above his head; elbows together, hands open, fingers spread. He gathers the ball, bringing it back tightly into his chest. Three times he does it. The thump of his boot, as it connects with the ball, grows louder the closer he comes to Dominic. He is about to kick his fourth when he sees him under the tree and stops. They are too far away to read each other's expression. Dominic takes a few steps forward, out from under the branches. Owen takes his kick. This time he does not watch it. The ball spins into the air and as it begins to drop, so does the rain, darkening the earth around their feet as the ball slams into the ground between them.

Cure Time

Giancarlo Gemin

Wherever Eileen was in the house the scrapes and snaps she heard coming from the kitchen were comforting. She always felt a little awkward in Lee's presence, even though he'd been in the house for more than two weeks. Perhaps it was the face mask that triggered a feeling of disquiet, as if his presence had to do with the extermination of pests. All the same, it was nice having him in the house and watching him work, though she only felt able to remain in his presence if she had something to do nearby, or feigned as such, like the tea she was now making that she didn't particularly want. She watched as he efficiently scored along a tile, then snapped off the excess making a satisfying crack. He swiftly pasted it with adhesive and placed it in position, using small plastic crosses that spaced the tiles evenly and poked out like crucifixes.

She had often chatted with him while he'd attached several tiles in a row, executed without hesitation, but it was the awkward areas that impressed her the most; she would notice he was approaching a pipe, or a corner, and the next time she was in the kitchen it would be resolved cleanly without any sign of difficulty. The tiles looked stylish and there was something reassuring about their precision. She could imagine her new kitchen as a centre spread in a home magazine, empty of people, with a plate piled with inviting croissants in the middle of the island. In contrast to the uniform order of the tiles, the openings for the power points were jagged and harsh and she used this to engage in conversation with Lee. He patiently explained that the plates of the double sockets would rest on top of the tiles, covering the openings, and demonstrated by holding one of the chrome power points in place. Eileen nodded, though she'd known that would be the case. She asked if he'd like another tea, then realised she'd offered when she'd entered the kitchen moments earlier. 'I was having one myself,' she added, flicking on the kettle and gazing out into the garden. While she waited she asked if there would be enough tiles, and without looking up Lee assured her there were plenty, and then added, 'It'll all be finished tomorrow.'

Eileen was surprised by the spike of disappointment she felt. 'What about the grouting?'

'Oh, that doesn't take long. They'll be cured in a few hours.'

'Cured?'

'Dried,' he said.

'Well... I'm very pleased,' she said. 'It's looking like a showroom kitchen. I can imagine it...' She laughed. 'I was going to say in a magazine.' His eyes smiled above his mask. She could think of nothing else to ask so she left him alone and made her way up the stairs.

Lee wasn't particularly talkative but she wondered if he was as taciturn with everyone. She went into the spare room where she had set up her laptop while the kitchen was being modernised. She gazed around as she waited for the internet page to appear. It was a room that was infrequently used, but always ready for an overnight visit by her daughter, Claire, or granddaughter, Suzy. Eileen had had it brightly decorated in a pale rose as well as installing a fitted wardrobe, though it stood empty aside from a duvet and pillows that were still in the packaging. She had purchased a photograph of a field of sunflowers that was split into three separate sections. She thought it was an uplifting picture. In fact, it was probably wasted in the spare room, and she decided she would move it to her bedroom to greet her in the morning. Perhaps she could ask Lee to hang it up, as she noticed that the three sections were not exactly in line. It was at that moment she had a feeling of foreboding, like opening the front door to a policeman. She listened for a few seconds until she heard the expected scrapes from downstairs, then she logged onto the dating website, keen for the distraction.

Her three-month subscription was coming to an end, though most of it had been wasted, because during the lockdown she couldn't have met anyone even if she had arranged a date. The confinement had been a further, unjust obstacle that felt like a spiteful turn of fate after she'd been brave enough to join the website in the first place. The last time she'd met anyone who had piqued her interest was the previous Christmas, when the consequences of a pandemic were unimaginable. The evening in the pub had started off so well, when she and Karen had begun a conversation with the three men on the adjacent table. It was not often that Eileen met someone with whom she felt comfortable, but it was easy talking to David, whom, she guessed, was in his mid-fifties. He had nice teeth, and was well built, like Lee. His fingernails were clean and Eileen noticed a tasteful ring, which was not on his married finger; it was a small bronze coin in a gold setting. She had liked his smart-casual dress sense – a long-sleeved, burgundy polo shirt, which was neatly tucked into his cream, khaki chinos, and he wore suede Chelsea boots. She had flattered herself that David was chatting her up, at least until Karen had interrupted. Eileen had sensed her watching and listening. 'Guess how old she is?' Karen had said. The conversation was cut dead and Eileen felt herself blush, though it wasn't the question that bothered her so much as the interruption. 'That's put me on the spot,' said David. 'You don't ask a lady her age, do you?' Eileen had smiled, trying to cover her embarrassment, but at the same time she was curious to know what he would guess.

'She's a granny,' Karen added.

Eileen's embarrassment turned to a flush of heat. She was proud of her figure and her looks, but it was still a private matter, and it was up to her to give out that information if she chose to. She had the feeling that David now seemed uncomfortable. 'Fifty-two?' he said. Eileen smiled and was about to change the subject when Karen promptly announced that Eileen was sixty-four. David looked surprised. In fact, Eileen thought she saw a glimmer of concern pass over his face. They continued chatting, but as a group rather than just the two of them. Eileen tried to avoid looking at David, even if she felt his eyes were upon her, and then later, when they all got up to leave, David had asked for her mobile number. She turned him down, but felt an immediate sour regret, like a sharp pain peaking and fading. Her quick, curt reply still stung with its recollection. Why couldn't she have simply changed her mind? She could have approached him outside in the car park, but instead she'd got into her car with Karen. She wanted to catch his eye as he drove out. She could have smiled, warmly, but he didn't even glance her way.

'Why didn't you give him your number, then?' Karen asked.

'He wasn't my type,' she'd replied, but the words felt dry in her mouth. Karen thought he was very attractive and wondered out loud what Eileen thought was wrong with him.

'Well, why didn't you give him *your* number?' Eileen replied, her frustration spilling out.

'He didn't ask me for it, did he?' Karen said.

No. He didn't, thought Eileen, but the momentary satisfaction turned as sour as the regret that still remained. They had argued. A full-on confrontation. That horrible rush of a thing, and Eileen drove on to a roundabout too fast, causing the wheels of her car to shriek. When they arrived at Karen's house Eileen stopped the car dead, as if a traffic light had suddenly turned red. Karen hurried to get out and accused her of being 'way too sensitive' before she slammed the car door. Eileen still felt a knot in her stomach at the missed opportunity. She couldn't deny that she liked the fuss about her appearing younger than her years, but she expected a certain etiquette. If only David had waited for the right moment and hadn't asked for her number so publically.

She scrolled down the profiles of the dating website. She was quick to spot new arrivals, and today a gentleman calling himself 'Man-Alive' had appeared. He was fifty-six, or said he was fifty-six – she was convinced everyone lied about their age, as she had done, simply because when she'd looked at men her age she had not been able to find one that she found attractive. After all, if she could look after herself, why couldn't they? 'Man-Alive' wrote that he was divorced, with two grown-up sons. He liked all the usual things: cinema, eating out, dancing, football, and was part of a tenpin bowling team. Eileen was glad it wasn't outdoor bowls as that had associations with retirement and the elderly, but tenpin bowling was a fun and youthful activity. She was doubtful of the reference to dancing. He was probably trying to impress. He'd ended his profile, *'Perhaps you'll be intrigued to find out just how alive I am?'*. She clicked on his photo. She expanded it, but the pixels blurred, denying her a closer inspection. All the same, he seemed nice-looking. She was disappointed that there was just the one photograph of him, as she offered three on her profile. One was a selfie she'd taken with her phone held high over her head. Another was of her dressed in a blue sequinned dress with a purple feather boa for a New Year's Eve party. It had been taken three years before, but Eileen thought it would demonstrate that she liked a night out and that she could be glamorous and fun. The third photograph was taken by Suzy when they'd been shopping together and had afternoon tea. It had been Eileen's treat for her granddaughter. The photo showed Eileen holding the teacup with her little finger sticking out, and her head tilted coquettishly next to a tier of cakes.

It often crossed her mind that someone she knew might spot her profile on the site, though this was outweighed by the prospect of meeting someone. She found it a great source of excitement, even if she dreaded the thought of being rejected, like the woman she'd once seen on a television dating programme. She was a confident woman of sixty-five, or so she said. She seemed to be getting on well with the charming, silver-haired man with whom she had been matched, but when it came to the moment when they were asked if they would like to see each other again, he'd said, 'Maybe as friends. I didn't feel a spark.' Eileen felt the woman's pain, as sharp as a slap. It had been so promising, then to be rejected and on national television was just inviting someone to do something drastic, or at least condemn them to a reclusive existence. Eileen imagined millions of viewers up and down the country laughing, but she was left feeling tense and troubled, as if she had been in the woman's place. She felt exposed in her own lounge and flicked through channel after channel, in an effort to get away from her rejected self.

She opened her profile and read it again, though by now she almost knew it by heart. '*I enjoy good company and stimulating conversation, and whilst I love a fun night out, I equally enjoy being in on a cold, winter's night, curled up and watching a good film on the TV'*. It was not true. To be in on a Friday or Saturday night, in particular, exaggerated her loneliness, especially during the long cruel nights of lockdown. *'I love going to the theatre, a concert or a gallery'*, she wrote, and yet she couldn't recall a time when she'd been to any sort of show or concert in the last five years. She had visited a gallery when she'd gone to London on an organised daytrip, which included a guided tour of the National Gallery. She had enjoyed the atmosphere of the beautiful, high-ceilinged rooms and the hushed reverence of people viewing the paintings. She'd listened keenly to her group's guide talking about the artists and had tried to concentrate on each of the paintings. She suddenly found herself alone, separated from the others. Her interest vanished as she raced from room to room trying to find the coach party, panicking at the possibility of being stranded in such a large and unfamiliar city. She had regretted going on her own, and on the return trip she was sitting with a woman who had chatted about her family as if she'd been asked for the smallest detail, and so during a pause in the chatter Eileen had pretended to fall asleep.

'Hello!'

The call from downstairs made her jump. She went out on to the landing and saw Lee at the bottom of the stairs looking up at her. 'I'm done for today,' he said. 'I'll finish the grouting tomorrow and put in all the sockets. I've put in one so you can boil the kettle.'

'Okay. Great,' she said as she made her way down.

He raised a hand. 'Don't worry, I'll let myself out.' He opened the front door. 'See you tomorrow.' She was going to thank him for his hard work, even though she must have done so a few dozen times. There was a gentle click as the front door closed. She watched him pull away in his van and then returned to the kitchen. Her pleasure at its gleaming, showroom look was tempered with disappointment that Lee was gone, and the way he seemed to hurry out. She looked over the last section that had been completed, searching for any irregularity, or a spacing that stood out, but she saw none. The house was quiet. She made the effort to try and listen for something, anything. The silence seemed complete, and then she noticed a mug containing an unused tea bag beside the kettle. It was the tea she had begun to make for herself earlier. She had switched on the kettle and talked to Lee about the power points. She'd boiled the water, but then absent-mindedly left it unfinished. What must he have thought? She flicked on the kettle again, and as she waited the trepidation returned. It was heavier now, and she looked around, searching for a clue to its cause. She made a conscious effort to finish making the tea, and then went back upstairs where 'Man-Alive's' profile was still on the laptop screen. His eyes were kind, she thought, and she clicked on the 'send a message' icon. The cursor flashed on the empty text box, waiting for her to write. She had written to a few men before; one had answered, but had been overly familiar and cheeky. Some others had not responded, which always rankled her. She closed the message box. 'Later,' she promised herself and logged into Facebook.

Her granddaughter had helped her set up her page, and Eileen had soon become addicted to trawling the pages of people she knew. After only a few days she had decided to ration her time because one evening she became aware that it had grown dark outside and four hours had slipped by. She had sat there feeling something that bordered on self-loathing, but since that time she was still unable to stop herself checking on Lenny's page, though it left her unsettled and even a little ashamed. Her daughter, Claire, had contact with him and was among his list of friends. When Eileen had seen his page the first time it had sent chills through her: to be able to peer into his life so easily and look through his photos; to see his home, and his children, like the group photo which included Claire among her half-siblings. She could see a strong likeness of her daughter in two of the three children Lenny had fathered after Claire. They had the same well-defined nose and his eyes, of course. His children looked happy, but the smile on Claire's face in the group photo seemed forced. Eileen found it all too easy to move from Lenny's page to those of his son and other daughters; a virtual family tree connected to her. Lenny was frequently active on his page. There would be new photographs which were always greeted with lots of likes and comments. His new girlfriend, Terri, who could not have been very much older than Claire, posted lots of selfies as well as photos with Lenny. She had two children herself and was constantly flaunting pictures of them – the virtual family extended ever further. There were photographs of him at a football match with his handsome son; a night out in a pub, holding up a glass of beer, and another as he stood at a microphone singing on a karaoke night – that one had thirty-seven 'loves', including one from Claire, and comments like, 'Still got it, Dad!' with a line of animated, laughing Emojis. She thought Lenny's semi-detached home, in the background, looked a little shabby. A few years before, he had invited Eileen to be friends and she'd ignored the invitation. The expected remonstrations from Claire never came. She made the effort to ask after Lenny whenever she knew Claire had met up with him and her siblings, but Claire was never particularly talkative about him. Eileen had to admit he was still handsome. He had put on weight, of course, but his eyes were still a deep brown. Those same eyes looked back at her now. She fantasised that her younger self was someone else – she had not been that unlucky young woman who had fallen pregnant. It was a soothing self-deception.

She opened her own Facebook page and scrolled down her posts until she saw her tribute to Brian. It was a post she had written the week after his funeral. The picture was one she had taken on the deck of a riverboat cruise in Hungary. Brian had been loyal and dutiful. If she suggested a day out he would agree to it. He had tried so hard to make her happy, and for that she was grateful, though she knew she had been moody and bossy with him. He never complained, but if only he'd kept trim, and if only she hadn't needed to remind him to take a shower, and if only he'd eaten more slowly and delicately. He would have been ideal, if, if, if. When he'd had the heart attack she was overwhelmed with remorse. She punished herself with the thought that she had contributed to his death. He'd been rushed into hospital and she was with him the moment he had died. He was staring at her as they attempted to resuscitate him. She forced herself to smile, but he didn't smile back. His gaze became fixed and his mouth opened, making him look almost gormless. She wondered about that look – his last thought. 'I love you, Brian,' she'd said, though she had rarely said it to him in their years of marriage. The nurse told her that he would have heard, but Eileen felt she was just trying to console her and ease the guilt that must have been etched on her face.

She got to her feet and opened the window. She sucked in the sharp, cold air. She saw her mother's stony expression when Eileen told her Lenny had left her. A look that said, *What did you expect?* Her father had helped and supported her, and then Brian, of course. He had 'come to the rescue' as her mother had put it. It was only from the moment that Brian had entered the scene that her mother became a grandmother and a nanny to Claire. She closed the Facebook page and shut the laptop. The unease returned again, like something urgent that couldn't be brought to mind.

Downstairs she looked around the nearly finished kitchen. She touched the tiles and pulled at one of the last to have been attached, but it was stuck firm. She took a knife from a drawer and wedged it behind the tile. The blade bent and the tile suddenly flew off the wall and broke on the floor. She slipped the knife behind the next one and it too broke away. She clenched her teeth, as tile after tile was broken off making harsh and offensive noises, until she reached a tile that resisted. The glue held and then the handle of the knife snapped from the blade. She stared at the blotches of dried adhesive; an irregular, ugly patchwork. She turned and walked over the broken tiles towards the front door. She glanced up the staircase and back down the hallway towards the kitchen. She put on her shoes and slipped on her coat. When she opened the front door she heard a siren in the distance. She waited for it to die away, then stepped out and shut the door. She pulled the bands of the mask over her ears and adjusted it over her nose. As she started to walk away the fear gradually began to fade.

Half Moon, New Year

Joshua Jones

— Get off me! Get the fuck off me!

He lies in a crumpled mess amongst shards of smashed glass and cigarette butts. Spilled booze drenches his skinny blue jeans. Makes it look like he's pissed himself. Maybe he has. The pocket of his white shirt is ripped and hanging by a thread. He's holding his hands up in front of his badly beaten face, the hands scuffed, palms embedded with grit. His brow is bust open and the cheekbone plummed, already beginning to swell. There's blood rushing the gap between nose and upper lip. The bottom lip is torn up bad too. His head is turned away towards the floor. He spits out a bubble of snot and blood, a subtractive mix of yellowish green and bloodstone red. The bubble bursts before it hits the ground. Danny Jenkins is pulled away from the boy on the floor by a mass of hands and screams. Disembodied voices howling what the fuck! Get off him! They sound far away, obscure. He stops trying to kick the boy and tries to find his feet on the alcohol-slicked floor.

It was raining and had been all night; chattering on the roof over the beer garden. Weather doesn't stop the drinking. The girls, in their skirts and makeup, flirt with the boys, squeeze up to them for warmth and for a packet of crisps. The boys,

101

in return, don't mind. They roll cigarettes for the girls — who don't want to smoke, not really, but maybe it'll warm them from the inside — asking them how the hell can they roll with those massive fake nails? The boys whose parents can afford to buy them expensive winter coats wrap them around the shoulders of the girls. These coats are SuperDry and North Face, the shirts Ralph Lauren or Levi, or else they wear River Island T-shirts a size or two too small to show off the muscles they're trying to develop. These muscles are filled with water and protein shake, but the girls say: yeah, they're massive. Look at you. You look huge. And so, so strong.

No one wants to admit they're cold. They all start the night hugging their knees or with their arms crossed in front of their chests, huddled as close as they can to the dented patio heaters without making their discomfort apparent. They drink their pints quickly, so their teeth won't chatter. Many of the girls can keep up with the boys, and the boys know it, but not all of them like beer or cider. Some of them want cocktails, with real fruity flavours unlike the artificial blackcurrant in their Dark Fruits cider. But they can't afford them, especially now with Christmas just gone. When the boys offer them a drink, they choose what they want — what they actually want — and savour it. Boys make fun of boys for drinking cocktails, or any drink that isn't piss coloured. Call them ponces. No one cares, though, not really. It's all jest and festive spirit. It's *banter*. And as the night goes on, the girls inch away from the patio heaters, their cheeks tipsy-flushed under their blush. It's New Year's and it beats being at home.

It has been a pretty good night. The corrugated plastic roof, in all its bird shit and glory, keeps them dry. Plus, the sound of the rain helps to construct an atmosphere where people feel cosy. While the boys just sort of stand around, talking about the Scarlets vs. Swans game and whatever else boys talk about, the girls open up. Talk about Christmas dinner and Boxing Day leftovers, happy younger siblings and Pandora rings transitions to — as the girls inch closer together across the wooden benches — conversations of family arguments and tensions at home. One girl complains about her bratty younger sister who threw a tantrum because she didn't get a Crosley record player. And another girl's dad is, like, a total dick when he drinks whisky, and he'd started drinking really early, before lunchtime, so by the time dinner was ready he had a look on his face, you know? And the gravy wasn't right, and the roasties weren't crisp enough, and Mum was in tears. And that night he sat at the table, alone, drinking, while everyone else's families sat around the TV or playing games. Here, the girl chokes back a sob, and the other girls cluster around her, dabbing gently at her tears so she doesn't streak her mascara, and she tells them that on Boxing Day morning she woke up to find her brand-new house plant, a Christmas gift, its stems snapped in half.

This is the scene inside the Half Moon pub: older men and women sit around rickety tables with sticky tops, perch on stools around the bar; couples around the pool table, their children at home, not mentioned. The TV is on, next to the darts board, the BBC presenter standing in front of crowds, the London Eye behind her, describing the atmosphere as electric, and lively. When a man goes outside for a smoke he nods at the young people, says something like:

    — Bloody cold, init? You having a good night?

    — Yeah, good thanks, yeah. Yours?

    — Sound, mate, yeah. Sound.

    And he stands in the doorway, listening to the jabber, puts out his cigarette and goes back in without saying a word. Or if it's an older lady she chats to the girls, says how beautiful they look, just bloody lush they all are, and the girls invite her to sit with them and she says don't mind me, love, don't mind me, and clip-clops back into the warmth. When the countdown begins the young people rush in and they all stand there, everyone intermingled and chuffed and arms around shoulders. They cheer and clap as the fireworks go off over the Thames in HD and the music plays. Everyone downs their drink and sings Auld Lang Syne out of tune, and no one knows the words, but it doesn't matter. A few tear up then and laugh it off, say they get emotional when they drink, but really, they are glad to have made it another year. And the new one will be a good one. They know it. They'll wish it into existence.

This is where Danny comes in through the heavy front door, another boy holding him up, both sodden and dripping and freezing cold. The other boy looking vaguely pissed off, the sort of look that says he's not having the best night but is trying to salvage it. And Danny, Danny is fucked. His eyes hard and unfocussed, his jaw clenched, unclenched, clenched. Everyone turns to look at them as they come through the door, the way people do when anyone enters a room. Danny tries to square up to them, unable to focus on anyone. His friend smiles, embarrassed. Their trainers squelch as the floor sticks to them and they cross the bar. The friend orders two Cokes and the barman asks is Pepsi okay, yeah? And the friend says yeah that's fine, whatever yeah.

By now the room has regained its composure. The music flows and so do the drinks. The atmosphere is merry and celebratory despite the two boys bursting in. There are toasts of Iechyd Da! to health, to family, to the New Year. Someone challenges another to a game of pool as they rummage through their pockets for a 50p coin for the table. Danny slumps over the bar and his friend pulls him up by the shoulder. Makes him sip the Pepsi, apologises to the bar staff when he slaps the glass down hard and sticky, cold Pepsi swamps the bar. No one says anything. They don't want to upset the mood.

The young ones trickle out into the smoking area and the cold, resume their positions around the patio heaters. Arms and legs folded, toes curled in their boots and heels and trainers. Cigarettes are slowly rolled by hands red-raw, the paper licked by tongues sneaked past chattering teeth. Everyone's sufficiently drunk enough now to freely complain about the cold, all bravado melted away. Danny and his friend follow them out to the smoking area. The friend thinks the fresh air might clear Danny's head.

— Alright? Mind if we join you? the friend asks, sheepishly.

They say of course, join them! They all converge closer together on the already coveted bench space. And the boys ask him if he saw the Boxing Day rugby match. Danny glares into the middle distance as if to pick a fight with thin air, aggressively silent and saying nothing as the friend discusses the tries and penalties and performances of individual players.

— Hey Dan, what do you reckon of Samson Lee's game? the boys ask, trying to get him involved.

His jaw clenches, unclenches, clenches. He says nothing, staring at something no one else can see.

— Not very talkative tonight, is he? one of the boys says in a taunting tone.

The friend quickly picks up the conversation to fill the awkward space. He sits as near to the heater as he can, his knees touching the metal base. His shirt is damp and he shivers, chains cigarettes for warmth. When the conversation lulls, one of the girls asks the friend where's he been that night.

— We'd been to Spoons first to meet up with our mates, but it went pretty dry pretty quickly. It's cheap yeah, but who wants to drink in a pub where there's no music? The others nod in agreement, take drags and sip their drinks. Someone goes to the bar, someone else offers to go with them. Two of the boys are having a heated discussion about this year's John Lewis Christmas advert. Danny sips his drink, the glass loose in his hand.

— So then we all went to Met Bar and that was alright.

— Must have been packed, was it?

— Proper packed, yeah, stood out in the rain for ages waiting to get in. But yeah, it was good. Decent atmosphere and all that. But then we had to leave 'cause we got chucked out, thanks to this one here. He jabs a thumb at Danny, who is now glaring at the friend.

— Why? What'd he do?

— Knob as usual, had to start a fight, didn't he? Had to leave then, thrown out by the bouncers.

— Fuck off now, isi? Danny says to the friend.

The friend shrugs, downs the dregs of his drink and gets up to go to the bar without asking Danny if he wants a refill. The girls turn around and begin talking between each other, feeling uncomfortable in Danny's presence. He slouches with his back against the brick wall, making no effort to ease the tension in his muscles.

Two boys and the friend return from the bar, their hands like claws around the glasses clutched to their chests, spilling foam and laughing. People come and go to the toilet for a piss or to do a bump. There's a smash followed by a euphoric wave of Waheey! from inside the pub. One girl says she has to go, her mum's waiting up for her, and all the other girls gets up to kiss her on the cheek, say they'll do something soon, before she goes back to university for the next semester. There are hugs and lots of Happy New Year's, babes. Someone, a boy, offers to walk her home, but she says she only lives a street away. And then she leaves through the smoking area, into the car park and down the road. Danny's friend sits down with a fresh pint and silently hands one to Danny, holding it in the air while he finds his unsteady grip. They sit in silence, not facing each other. A girl gets off her phone with a *fuck sake*! and jams it into her clutch bag. One of the girls closest to her asks:

— What's wrong, babes?

— Can't get hold of Big Dave again, mun. I know it's New Year's and he's busy, but he said he'd be here an hour ago.

— Ah, fuck, that's annoying. I'm running out too.

Danny's friend overhears the conversation and pauses mid-roll, a cigarette filter in his mouth.

— You talking 'bout Big Dave? I've got some here if you want?

The two girls come over to where Danny and the friend are sitting. The boys watch them, annoyed that the girls would rather give them attention. One of the older men, stood in the corner with a smoke, turns his head but doesn't say anything.

— Shhhh! Talk a little quieter, yeah?

— Right, yeah, sorry. Do you want some them?

— Aye, go on, ta. Car park?

— Let's go for it. You coming, Danny? the friend asks.

Danny shakes his head, his face like uncut stone. He watches the friend and the two girls make their way through to the car park, stepping over feet and handbags, saying they'll be back in a minute when someone asks them where they're going. Someone asks Danny if he's alright and he nods once, takes a big gulp of lager. The friend and the two girls crouch behind a car. Danny can't see them except their heads, but he knows the friend will pour a sliver of coke from the baggie onto his knuckle, then he'll offer to do the same for the girls, as if to be a gentleman, but the girls will take the bag from his outstretched hand and pour their own quantity. It will be a small amount too, as to not take the piss, but maybe a little more than the friend's portion, to help see them through the night. They lift the knuckle to their nose and close one nostril with their finger, and all at once they inhale, in comradery.

When they return, they're rubbing their noses with the back of their hand, stretching the skin around the bridge with their fingers to ease the sinuses. The friend plonks down on the seat next to Danny, grinning widely. There's a new intensity in his eyes, the muscles around them hard. The friend pulls a packet of gum from his pocket and slips a piece in his mouth. He makes sure the translucent bag of white powder is firmly sealed. Danny silently, slowly, lifts a finger in the air. The friend looks at him. Danny says nothing, looks him in the eyes. The friend is chewing the gum in a frenzy. He pulls the bag back out of his pocket and unseals it, holds it out to Danny, who dabs a finger in the powder, then lifts it to his mouth and rubs it into his gums.

Conversation resumes, and Danny eases up, joins in. When someone says they watched the *Home Alone* films for the first time over Christmas he says what the fuck? You've never seen *Home Alone* before?! And when the girls talk about New Year resolutions, about wanting to start back at the gym and try a new fad diet, try to shift some of the Christmas weight, he says nah, no need. You're fit as it is. They say thanks, laugh dryly, shift uncomfortably in their seat. Danny shrugs it off. He offers to buy the friend a drink, the first time since they arrived at The Half Moon. And Danny goes off without offering to buy anyone else a drink. The friend sits back in his seat, relaxed but intense, eyes darting back and forth from face to face and ears tuning in and out of the conversations around him. His stomach is churning but not in an entirely bad way; this next drink will have to be the last.

Danny reappears in the doorway with two full glasses in his hands, walks across the decking and next thing the friend knows, Danny is on the ground. The glasses smash on impact and the sweet smell of cider fills the air as the golden liquid and foam flows into the gaps between the planks of wood. There's a cheer of Waheey! from inside the pub. The girls scream and everyone in the smoking area jumps at the sound of glass smashing, and the mass of flesh and fabric slamming the ground. They lift their feet and bags off the floor on to the bench, so as not to be soaked in the spilled drink. The boys laugh in unison, a chorus of cruelty.

The friend and one of the girls rush to help Danny to his feet but he's up before they can get to him, his cheeks flushed, lips pulled back over his teeth, and before anyone can stop him he pulls his fist back and socks the boy closest to him on the jaw. Danny grabs at the boy's shoulder and punches him in the stomach, once, twice, three times, four. Danny wrestles the other boys off him with a strength that has built through the night from the drinking and the drugs. There are screams and shouts to get off him. There's a sound of ripping cloth. The boy is shouting get off me, get off me! He tries to push Danny back so he can get a punch in but can't, Danny hitting too fast and too strong. The boy curls up on himself, his hands in front of his face. Danny pushes the boy's hands away, the bundles of arms and hands unable to keep him from the boy.

There's the sound of knuckles hitting soft skin and muscle. The boy's cries of pain and shouting for Danny to stop. Two girls are crying. One of them starts beating on Danny's arm and pushing him but he doesn't notice. Danny's face frozen in a snarl, his eyes stony. One of the boys pulls the girl away, tells her to not get involved. Danny starts to tire, and the boys manage to pull him back, not before he knees the boy in the stomach and drops him to the ground.

— Get off me! Get the fuck off me!

The boy lies in a crumpled mess amongst shards of glass and cigarette butts. Spilled booze drenches his jeans. He's holding his hands up in front of his face, the hands scuffed, grit embedded in the palms. The brow is bust open and the cheekbone plummed, already beginning to swell. There's blood rushing the gap between nose and upper lip. The bottom lip is torn up bad too. His head is turned away towards the floor. He spits out a bubble of snot and blood, a subtractive mix of yellowish green and bloodstone red. The bubble bursts before it hits the wooden decking. Danny is pulled away from the boy on the floor by hands and screams. Disembodied voices howling what the fuck! Get off him! They sound far away, obscure.

— The fuck, Danny? What the hell you doing?

— The cunt fucking dropped me! I know he did! He stands there, his chest rising and falling, drenched in sweat despite the cold.

— No one dropped you, you fucking idiot. You tripped and fell!

— Nah, fuck off. He did. I saw him put his foot out.

— Danny no one tripped you up, you freak! one of the girls shouts at him.

He turns to face her, his hands still tightly balled into fists.

— I'm so sorry, everyone. I'm really sorry. He's been like this all night, I'm fucking taking him home, I'm sorry.

The friend grabs Danny by the shoulders and pushes him to the door, apologising the whole way. Danny doesn't put up any resistance as he's pushed through the door, shocked faces following them. There's a boy with a dustpan and brush and a puzzled look on his face, who squeezes up against the wall to let Danny and the friend push past. The friend pushes him through the pub so quickly no one has a chance to get a proper look and wonder what the bloody hell is going on.

The air in the smoking area had been thick with cigarette smoke; the inside of the pub stuffy with bodies emanating heat, packed from wall to wall, the radiators on full blast. Out here on the street, the air is so cold it burns Danny's split knuckles. It begins to rain again, with him and the friend on the doorstep of The Half Moon. The rain drips through a hole in Danny's jeans. Must have happened when he fell. His palms are grazed and sting in the cold. The friend won't look at him. His head is pounding.

— You're a prick, you know that, don't you?

The friend is breathing heavily, on the verge of shouting. Danny doesn't answer, bends down to inspect the badly bleeding knee through the hole in his jeans.

— That's it then? Just not ganna answer me?

Danny sighs, his brain beating a drum against his skull. He looks across the roundabout outside the pub, at the Capel Als church that looms over the road; separated by a cast iron fence that may have once been painted gold, now faded to a sort of beige. He remembers trooping down the hill as a child in primary school under the guidance of their teachers, uniformed under their little coats, to sing Christmas carols at the chapel. Danny and his friend would sit in the balcony, singing the carols and hymns in silly voices, like Darth Vader or Batman, under their breaths.

— Do you remember when we were kids?

— The fuck you on about now, Danny?

— Do you remember when we were kids, and always had to sing there, every Christmas? Danny points at the chapel. Those were the best days of my life. Simpler then, init?

He lets his hand drop to his side. Laughter and music come faintly from inside the pub, a car beeps its horn in the distance. The rain, falling heavier now. He looks up and blinks away the rain.

— Shame there's no stars out tonight.

— I can't be fucked with this, Danny. I'm done. Go home, will you?

Danny watches as the friend disappears down a turning. He begins to walk up the hill in the opposite direction, past Capel Als, the warm glow from the Half Moon's windows fading with every step. He wonders if the friend meant what he said. For the first time that night he notices his shirt is soaked through; with rain mostly, sweat and alcohol too. There's blood on the collar and the cuffs.

Y Castell

Chloë Heuch

It took us ages to get there and then, could I find a parking space? So many bloody tourists. Cai needed the toilet. Again. And Osian and Luke were really starting to get on my nerves, bickering over whose football team was the best. Then they saw the castle.

It is impressive. I'd been promising the boys we would visit since, well, forever. But it was more than an hour along the coast, and their dad always had something on – drinking with his mates usually.

You come through the town, only able to see the towers sticking up with the flags waving about, then the road takes you past it. The walls loom up from the moat, walls so high your eyes have to travel up to find the sky.

Not that my eyes could as I was still looking for a parking space at that point. But you get the picture.

'It's massive!' Luke yelled in my ear as he lent forward in his seat.

'Put your belt back ON,' I snapped as I spotted someone with reverse lights on about to exit their space.

'Woah,' Cai murmured.

'It's just a stupid lump of rock.' Osian folded his arms and looked the other way.

'Too old for fun now, eh Osh?' I glanced at him in the passenger seat as I pulled the car into the empty parking place. His arms were crossed and his brow furrowed. The eldest of my boys. At twelve, he still had some softness of the boy about his face, but his body was too big for itself, growing so fast and so tall. Just like his dad.

I bought a ticket from the pay and display. It was a bright but blustery day, with a quick wind that tried to steal the ticket from my fingers. After dragging Cai into the public loo (20p?!!) we finally made our way up the mottled stone steps, underneath the portcullis and through the giant entrance.

'One adult and three children, please.'

'That'll be £26.60 please.'

'Is that the family price?' I asked the lady in the ticket booth.

'Yes, it is a little cheaper than buying individually.'

I handed over the money as I eyed Cai and Luke. They had already squeezed past me into the great inner space beyond the entrance. They bounded onto the immaculate green grass, past the neat white sign that read DO NOT WALK ON THE GRASS.

'Lovely day for it.' She smiled at me as she returned my change and a leaflet with the layout of the castle on it. 'The falconry display starts at 12.'

'That's great. Thanks.' I smiled back. She had kind, patient eyes: a grey-haired old lady who had done her time with children, survived and come out the other side, who sat patiently all day in a portacabin and wore neat white blouses.

'Enjoy.' Her gaze moved beyond me to Osian, but he had turned his back on us and stuffed his earpods in again.

'Thanks.' Her smile was understanding as she brought her gaze back to me. Moving away, I felt my eyes prickle with tears. God, what was wrong with me?! I could do this. We were a family. I was their mum, like I'd always been. Just because – because HE wasn't with us, it didn't make any

114

difference. Steve wouldn't have been any help even if he was with us, I reminded myself.

'Come on Osh,' I tugged my eldest's arm. 'Cai, LUKE!' I shouted as I jogged to reach my two younger boys who were scrambling over a low wall – next to a sign that read DO NOT CLIMB ON THE WALLS. This was a test for myself. I could do single parent. I could do family outings. I could do normal. I could do it on my own.

The walls surrounded us. Granite grey reached up to the blue sky on all sides. The tops of the walls were walkways between each of the towers. I could see people strolling along. The only thing stopping them from falling a good thirty feet was the thinnest of metal barriers. Great. That would not stop my lunatic children from leaping off them at the first opportunity.

'Right. You must not go on the walls without me. Okay? No running on them and be careful on the stairs.'

'Yeah okay. Come ON mum.' Cai dragged me toward the sign marked DUNGEON.

**

'Wow,' I exclaimed, pointing out the display to Osian. 'They started building in 1384. Can you imagine? These stones are seriously old. There would have been no forklifts or cranes to help, would there?'

'What?' he said, pulling out his earpods.

I had dragged the kids inside one of the towers marked MUSEUM, while we waited for the falconry display. It was easier than trying to stop the younger ones from doing something crazy a hundred feet up a tower. I thought maybe Osian would find something to interest him. But it was the same response I'd been getting all summer: flat, uninterested.

I missed my boy; the one whose brown eyes would open in wonder when we showed him things: tractors, planes, birds. He'd had so much interest and curiosity in our great wide world. Now though, since the divorce, and even before it, he had retreated inside the walls of himself. The portcullis was well and truly down.

'I was just saying – how old it is…the castle…' I faltered under that dead gaze of his and I looked away. I felt tears again trying to beat me, trying to escape. 'Come on,' I managed. 'Let's go see the birds.' He shrugged my hand off his arm and walked out into the brightness, chewing the edge of his lip.

A crowd was gathering around a white cordon on the grass in the centre of the castle where two handlers stood. One waited at the far end by a tall perch. The second was a young woman with a mike attached to her polo shirt. She had a large leather glove on one hand and balanced upon it was a small bird of prey. She smiled and began to address the audience. Cai and Luke wriggled forward through the throng. Osian stayed beside me at the back.

'Welcome to the Castle Falconry display,' the woman explained. 'Among the birds you will see today are a variety of raptors that would have been used by medieval lords as entertainment and sport. This here is Arthur.' She raised her arm into the air to show us the sharp beaked bird, whose quick eyes took us all in. 'Anyone know what kind of bird he is?'

A few hands went up and someone at the front called out 'Peregrine Falcon.'

'Correct.' The handler smiled. 'Peregrines have a blue-grey back like Arthur here—' She stopped to put a small titbit of meat between the finger and thumb of the glove. The bird wrenched at it using his beak. 'He also has the barred underparts and a blackish head. Of course, peregrines are renowned for their speed…'

Cai and Luke were still, for once, mesmerised by the handler and the peregrine as she walked backwards and forwards along the cordon.

The younger ones were less affected by the divorce. At least, they hadn't shown any major upset. Cai had started wetting the bed again when Steve moved out, and Luke had asked lots of questions. But that seemed to have passed now and they'd accepted it. Mum and Dad didn't love each other anymore. That's all there was to it.

I kept my opinions to myself as much as I could. For example, the fact Steve only loved himself and there was no room for anyone else in his heart. That he was a selfish bastard and would always let others down, no matter what. They still saw him every week: Tuesdays and Saturdays. But he was starting with the excuses already.

I watched the peregrine, who was now flying freely far above our heads. It seemed impossible he would ever return as he arced high above the crenellations, a boomerang shape against the blue. But he turned and bulleted back toward the lure. The male handler swung the lure in an arc and the peregrine almost caught it, but then swooped back up into the sky. Osian's eyes followed it.

I wondered if this new Osian would have appeared anyway to replace my lovely, sweet boy. If he was just the teenage version and that the changes I saw in him were inevitable. He'd be thirteen soon. Everyone kept telling me kids grew up quicker these days. Was this sullenness just part of growing up? Or was it my fault? Had I missed something? Should I have stuck with Steve until they were older?

The peregrine flew and dived again. Then the handler gave him the meat he longed for and he settled back on to the glove. She brought him right up to the cordon. Cai and Luke were straining to see. She knelt so they could take in the slate grey-blues and barred white of his feathers, the yellow talons that gripped her glove, the sharp, clever eyes.

'Beautiful, isn't he?' I said to Osian.

It took me a moment to register, but when I saw him bring his sleeve up to his eyes, it sunk in. Osian was crying.

'Love, what is it?' I leaned toward him, desperate to comfort him but he shrugged me off.

'Don't Mum.'

'Don't what?'

'Don't—' He lifted his hands and shook them, as though trying to free his fingers from a sticky cobweb. Then he looked at me. At last, he really looked at me. Proper eye contact. The first since what felt like forever. His marble eyes had softened and were wet with tears. He looked into mine.

'Mum—'

'What's wrong Osh?' I fought the impulse to put my arm around him.

There was a long pause. His eyes flickered over to the new bird of prey, a kite now, larger and more hunched on the handler's glove, like a covetous scrooge over his shred of meat.

Osian took a deep breath. 'I want to live with Dad.'

'What?'

'I want to live with Dad.' He said it louder, his gaze not wavering from mine.

'But – you do. Tuesdays and Saturdays.' I shook my head, not understanding what he meant.

'I want to live with him all the time. I don't…' His voice trailed off.

It was my turn for the tears to well up and spill over. It was my turn to wipe my eyes with the back of my sleeve. 'But why?'

'I just do.' He shrugged and put his hands in his pockets.

I wanted to say Steve put him up to this, just to hurt me. That his dad didn't really want him at all. My spite bubbled, forming into words, but... Osh. Sweet, lovely Osh. If I put that thought in his mind, it would flutter around inside him banging into reason, waking him in the middle of the night. Instead I asked, 'Does Dad know what you want?'

Osian nodded. I could hardly breathe.

He looked at me like he had never looked at me before: grown up, decisive, like he knew stuff I didn't. And I felt it all the way through me. He meant it and I would not be able to change his mind. He was not my little boy. He was his own person and this was his own decision and I had to let him make it. I was powerless against it. All of it: his dad, his influences, our life, the history of us, the family. This is what it had come to. Broken down into small pieces that could float away anywhere.

'Okay,' I said finally. 'If that's your decision. But I'll always be here for you.' I imagined myself like these old castle walls. Enduring. Always ready to protect him if he needed me. It would be his decision if he returned or if he flew on, out of sight.

'Thanks Mum.' He smiled and he hugged me. Proper hugged me, arms right round my waist and his head nuzzled into the crook of my arm.

I kept my arm round him as we watched the red kite soar into the blue sky, high above the castle, above us, above it all.

And then he dived.

The Truth is a
Dangerous Landscape

Susmita Bhattacharya

The gap year isn't something my family believes in.

'It isn't wise to waste the most important year of one's youth travelling around the world. Besides, there's no money set aside for that. Med school fees only.'

'No need to travel to India to find yourself – you're already from India. There's nothing to find there you don't already know.'

But here we are, the lot of us – in India. A sabbatical, our father convinces the relatives, this is what everyone in the UK does. So here we are. To get to know the desi family better. To get to know our roots.

My sister has failed her first year at med school. There are other secrets that we don't divulge to the relatives. The scars on her wrists are fresh, but everyone ignores them. They will fade by the time we return home. I've always wanted a gap year, but this isn't how I imagined it to be.

Summer evenings are drawn out here, usually scented with the bright pink and yellow shondhamoni flowers covering every inch of the garden verge. We lie back on the charpoy in our grandmother's courtyard and count the vultures lining up on the dead Sal tree across the road.

'There's something dying somewhere,' I say. My body is alert with the excitement of what is to come. I want to witness the vultures feed. There is a thrill to witnessing something so raw and visceral. Our middle-class street in Cardiff doesn't even boast of seagulls or crows. Only blue tits and chaffinches in people's landscaped gardens. 'It's got to be nearby. Look at how restless they are.'

'Hmmm.' My sister isn't interested. Her eyes are closed and I observe her nostrils flare and ease. Her eyelashes are caked with mascara, black smudges daubing her high cheekbones. This weather is not kind on make-up, but she refuses to accept that. I spit on my finger and attempt to wipe the marks off her skin, but she jerks back with such ferocity that I stare at her until she succumbs.

'What would you do if you got into something you can't get out of?'

'What do you mean?' I ask her. The vultures are now sweeping down from the tree and circling over the field across from our grandmother's house. The courtyard is filling up with the aroma of goat curry that's been cooking in the mud oven all day. It has become so overpowering that it's impossible for us to stop salivating. But it still has a couple more hours to reach that sublime state: of meat melting away from the bone, the potatoes almost falling apart, the caramelised gravy thickening in the iron pot.

She sits up and I see for the first time how tired she looks. I mean, not tired because of jet lag. Or tired because of the killing schedule at university. But a different kind of tired. Not the I've-failed-med-school tired. I'm anxious just looking at her. And very concerned. She's the sensible one, not one to get into trouble. Ever.

And she tells me. In such plain language, there is no argument, no twist to the story.

'This is sexual assault,' I say to her. 'He has taken advantage of you. Plain and simple.'

She shakes her head. 'But how can it be? I've let it happen.'

'Did he – did he go all the way?' I ask. But she shakes her head and closes her eyes. 'Thank god for that.'

'What would you do, Mira?' she asks me. And this is the question that plays on and on in my head.

What would you do, Mira? What would you do?

**

Here's what I would do:

I would not let anyone take advantage of me.

I would not allow any man to brainwash me with his sob stories.

I would not let him go scot free.

I would not let my family know what I had just gone through.

I would not want anyone to tell my family.

I would have to keep it quiet.

I would have no choice but to let him continue.

I would have to bear it silently until …

I would have to kill myself.

**

She had been trying to understand the methodologies that underpinned the epidemiological investigations of malaria and to describe the disease patterns in human populations, when he leaned forward and touched her hand. She didn't quite understand his action. Perhaps he was trying to stop her from speaking, to explain the methodology to her. Perhaps she was not making sense and so he reached out to make her shut up. She stopped speaking and he moved forward and kissed her firmly on the lips. When she bent back so far that her chair fell to the floor, and she hit her head hard on the threadbare carpet, he was just as shocked as she was.

He apologised fervently, his hands flapping about, his hair flopping over his eyes. Like a schoolboy who did not realise what he had done. He was sorry. He really was. She had rushed out of his office, leaving her laptop and bag inside. She had walked three miles to get back to her shared accommodation because she didn't have her wallet on her. And then she had sent a friend to his office – to collect her stuff.

**

'Let's go for a walk,' I say. I want to escape the confines of the courtyard where our grandmother is preparing the evening meal. She holds the black pot up with coconut husks as a substitute for oven gloves. The aunts are chopping up onions and chillies for the salad and cooking the chapatis.

We step out onto the road. Her hand is trembling when I take hold of it. Everything begins to make sense now. Her sudden withdrawal, her absence from family gatherings. Her falling ill constantly. Her failing biostatistics and epidemiology. It isn't easy when your father is a respected GP. And your mother is an obstetrician, bringing big, fat, healthy babies into the world. It will certainly not do to have a daughter fail medical school. And be a rape victim as well. It simply will not do.

'This has been going on for a while, hasn't it?'

She nods, her fingernails digging into my palm.

The vultures are circling above a ditch in the far end of the field. They swoop down, one by one, their wings stretching out darkly against the magenta sky, looking like pairs of hands stretched out to cup the sun. The bats streak through the sky, criss-crossing each other with frenzied precision. We can't go too far from home. It's not safe. Not for young women. Certainly not for young women with a foreign accent – we stand out in this small town in West Bengal and are ripe for picking. But I can't miss the dance of the vultures. What will they be feasting on while we feast on the goat curry? Probably the same thing. But I still want to see. My sister keeps walking. Once she's started talking, she will not stop.

'After failing his subjects, I went to see him again,' she is saying, striding purposefully across the field, dodging the goat pellets and cow dung. 'I wanted to know why he had failed me. And he explained to me, very patiently. Very kindly. And once again, he apologised for what had happened earlier.'

'The bastard,' I muttered. 'Trying to soften you up.'

'Well, he arranged for another tutorial. Told me that he could help me work on the assignment and resubmit. He told me to forget everything and start afresh. And I believed him. Actually, I was desperate to pass.'

'Why didn't you complain in the first place?' I was so angry I wanted to shake her. For being such an idiot. For being such an easy target.

She sighed and shook her head. 'You don't understand. I had nothing to complain about – at the beginning. He had said it had been a mistake. He was so close to tears, I felt sorry for him. And he did it again, and this time I didn't stop him.'

'That's how they operate – these men who know exactly how to throw the bait and bring in an unsuspecting woman into their trap.'

'How do you know?' she says.

'Well, you know.' I leave it at that.

I can't believe she is still sticking up for him. But those scars on her wrist tell me another story.

**

It was about six in the morning, and I was awakened by the thud-thud-thud of Dad racing downstairs, yelling indistinctly into his phone. A shallower thump-thump of Mum's footsteps trying to keep up with him. It was cold – the heating hadn't kicked in yet – and I struggled between wanting to burrow deeper into my duvet or rush out to see what had happened. Dad's panic-stricken voice left me with no choice. I ran downstairs and was confronted with a scene I never wish to see again in my life. Mum, in her nightdress, sobbing into a tea towel. She swayed from side to side while Dad barked into the phone.

'What's happened?' I rushed to her side and held her up. But she crumpled into my arms and whispered my sister's name again and again. Dad held his hand up.

'Let me listen to what they're saying,' he shouted at us. We bit our lips to keep from crying out. He scribbled something down. An address. A hospital. And then we were racing down the M4. I did not notice when the signs stopped being bilingual. I was hypnotised by the swishing of the wipers, the sulphur beams that lit up the bridge we were hurtling across.

**

We walked along the path that cut the field into two equal halves. One side was used by the local children – a cricket pitch and two football goalposts existed in perfect harmony. Often the boys playing the games got confused about what they were playing and joined the other sport in their state of heightened excitement. The other side was a wasteland where cowherds often brought their cattle to graze. It wasn't surprising to spot a jackal there, usually in a blur of movement. When it got dark, one heard them howling hukka-hua hukka-hua into the long, star-studded night.

It is forbidden to go out into the field after sundown. Not just for the scorpions and snakes that may lie in wait. More often, it was a human that caused more of a threat. Children abducted into the night. Women stripped of their jewellery and much more. An old man was once tied to the bark of a tree, his gold tooth pulled out, and was left to die. Such atrocities narrated as exciting stories over dinner – so far from our orderly lives. And yet, they don't seem that far.

'Dad has decided,' she said to me, taking hold of my hand. 'I cannot carry on studying – not at home anyway.'

'Then where?' I ask her, but I already know. He is on a mission here. To get her into a medical college in India. To have a safe and uneventful life far away from the wagging tongues and curious eyes.

'Here,' she says and turns away from the path. Perhaps she is tempting a scorpion to dig its sting into her. Or a snake to finish off her unfinished business. 'He wants me to leave my life as I know it and change the future for me. Just like that, everything will be okay.'

'Hey.' I pull her towards me. I am aware that we cannot continue down this path anymore. The boys are returning home from their games and soon it will be deserted. The sun has gone down, leaving a blush of gold above. The vultures look like paper cut-outs against the sunset as they careen down behind the trees. They are going in for their feast. I pull her towards the woods. Maybe we could get just a glimpse before turning away.

**

The ICU is not the place you want to see your sister. A mass of wires and pipes sprouting out from her. Her face obscured by the oxygen mask, breaths coming out loud and raspy. And her wrists – those delicate wrists – bandaged to look like boxing gloves. I stroked her arm with my little finger. The hair on her skin was standing on end. It was cold in there, and I wanted to hug her to keep her warm. But I didn't want to touch her either. An eyelash clung to her cheek and I bent down towards her face. I closed my eyes and made a wish. Then I blew on her cheek, ever so gently. The eyelash did not budge. I blew harder and she opened her eyes. She looked directly at me, her expression sliding from recognition to joy to fear. I looked away and noticed the eyelash had disappeared. I smiled. Because I knew my wish would now come true.

**

'You have to tell them the truth,' I say. I'm torn between watching the vultures feast and allowing her to witness it. She's in such a fragile state now, it's better she doesn't see them rip open the carcass. I can hear them screeching, and I see her flinch. I grab her arm and we turn back towards the house.

'He must be punished. He's ruined your life.'

I find myself shouting over the squawking birds, roosting in the trees around us. I see the night watchman waving frantically at us.

'Chalo, chalo,' he yells. He needs to lock the gates before he can settle in for the night with his bottle of country liquor. The housemaid always complains about him and his drunken leering when she must pass through the field at dawn to start work at the house. We go past his shed. It reeks like the urinal on the other side of the path, good lord, how did he manage to sit inside the entire night, enveloped in that stench?

'Go home quickly,' he says, giving us a salaam. 'It's not the jackals you need to fear. It's the witches that lurk among the trees. Look, one bit my ear off.'

127

He sticks his ear out at us, and sure enough, the lobe has been ripped off, leaving a jagged edge. We grab each other's hands, not sure if we fear the 'witch' or this red-eyed man in front of us. He smells of turpentine and bidi, and when he laughs, we see that his mouth is stained blood-red.

'The petni bit my ear off,' he whispers, looking around him with exaggerated care. 'When I refused to give her what she was after. I could do with a few rupees to protect myself from those witches.' His eyes linger on my breasts for a second before he bends his head in supplication.

'Pervert,' I mutter, pulling my dupatta higher up my body.

'Sorry,' my sister says. 'We don't have any cash on us.'

We sprint towards the gate, and can hear him snigger, quickly changing into a fit of coughing.

'Won't be long before he joins the petnis in the woods,' I say. My sister laughs for the first time, and I feel pleased that I made her do so.

**

Mum dressed us up as petnis once for Halloween. I wanted to go as the Wicked Witch of the West. My sister a zombie. But Mum wouldn't have any of it.

'We have enough ghosts and ghouls in our own traditions to choose from, why don't you go as one of those?' she said.

We screamed at the horror of the idea. We didn't want to dress up as some Indian ghosts and get laughed at. But Mum wrapped white saris round us and plonked silver wigs from Poundland on our heads. Our faces were whitened with talcum powder and a floury paste, eyes darkened with kohl and Dracula teeth covering red tongues dyed with food colour. We were allowed to wear lipstick, so that was a win. It wasn't so bad in the end. We looked terrifying – two petnis let loose in Cardiff.

We were quite a hit in the neighbourhood as well. Everyone complimented us on our ghostly get-up. Later we demanded a McDonald's meal and Mum gave in. She stuffed us into the back of the car and we drove to the nearest restaurant.

'Petnis don't eat burgers,' Mum laughed. 'They eat men. Chew them up and spit out their bones. You're such great petnis, you should win an Oscar or something.' She threw a french fry at us and burst out laughing.

We giggled as I transformed into a ghostly figure. An old hag with claws for fingers and a ketchup-stained grin.

'Whooooo, I'm coming to get you,' I cackled. 'Just wait and watch.' I chased Mum and my sister to the car and when we sat inside, she took a deep breath and leaned back into her seat.

'The two of you will haunt me for the rest of my life,' she said under her breath. I don't think I was supposed to hear that, so I didn't reply. She drove away and I packed that tiny moment of togetherness into my memory. It had been worth it in the end.

**

'Why don't you tell the truth to Dad and Mum?' She looks at me with such wide eyes, I fear they will pop out.

'Why lie that you tried to kill yourself because you failed your exams?'

'I would have also tried to kill myself if I'd just failed my exams.'

Again, her answer stupefies me. Surely this isn't the way forward? I observe the family settling down to eat. They are all our flesh and blood, but how distant they look. Strangers pretending to be united in the face of a disaster. The disaster itself a lie. They are talking excitedly of wedding proposals coming through the door each day for our cousin brother. They're discussing how to arrange for my sister's admission into medical college. They're discussing a future summer holiday to visit us in Cardiff.

We are welcomed to the table and my grandmother is serving the goat curry. To my father first – he is the esteemed son-in-law. Then to our uncles and cousin brother. My mother next, as she is the UK-returned daughter. The aunts wait with practised patience. They are busy passing the salad around, popping hot chapatis on plates and teasing our cousin to eat less, not to put on weight now when the prospective brides will come to look at him. I want to puke into the plate. All this seems so natural. Like nothing wrong has happened, it's all been whitewashed until we are all shiny, happy people.

My sister picks a piece of mutton and tears off a piece with her teeth. I think of the vultures feasting nearby. I think of the watchman drinking himself to oblivion. I think of the tutor, probably tucking into his Sunday roast on the other side of the world. Nobody gives a shit about what has happened to her. Nobody gave a shit about what had happened to me. I feel the bile rush up from the pit of my stomach and I rush towards the bathroom. Everything zooms in to that day. And I find it difficult to breathe.

**

Diwali parties at our house were like 'the event of the year' for my parents' friends. Mum always got our clothes and jewellery from India – which meant that we made that trip to my grandmother's in the summer holidays so that she could stock up on the party clothes. We were subjected to being measured by a creepy tailor, whose measuring tapes and fingers often brushed against certain parts of our bodies – all perfectly normal to everyone involved, it seemed. We'd have to parade in front of the family in our itchy and tight chaniya cholis – despite all the 'careful measuring', the tailor never seemed to get the fitting right.

After the three weeks spent in the horrid heat with nothing to do but read the *Readers' Digest* condensed novels again and again, we'd return home with suitcases crammed with silk saris and zardozi skirts and costume jewellery that could clothe probably half the Asian population in the city.

The Diwali party, when I was nine, was no different. Mum had cooked for an entire week. She actually took a week off work to stay home and prepare dishes that made the whole house smell of roasted spices and nostalgia. I would make sure my bedroom door was firmly shut, because I couldn't tolerate the strong aroma of the curries, especially on my school cardigans. My sister didn't have a choice because she'd have to help Mum with the cooking. She was a young lady now – and needed to learn to be useful in the kitchen.

They played cards in the lounge. The men drank whisky and laughed loudly, placing bets which grew to staggering amounts as the night wore on. The women sat in the dining room, or in the kitchen, helping with the cooking and serving, gossiping about someone's illicit affair or the lack of one. The children were usually sent up to my sister's bedroom to play. My sister locked herself in her room with the other teens. They didn't want the younger kids hanging around while they discussed – god only knew what. Nobody checked on us, so the boys knew they could use words like 'fuck' and 'chutiya' and get away with it. I hated being trapped in the bedroom with those kids, so I'd hide under the dining table and eavesdrop on even more colourful language and gossip that my mother and her friends exchanged in between sips of orange juice spiked with gin or vodka. I knew because they'd hide the bottles under the table, and I'd have to pull my knees tightly to my chest as the space underneath got lesser and lesser.

But that party – when I was nine – I decided not to sit under the table. The laughter was distracting me, and I really wanted to play on my new Nintendo 64. I sneaked into my father's study, where he kept the games console so he could keep an eye on the hours and minutes we spent playing games instead of studying.

I was so engrossed in my game that I didn't see someone enter the room and shut the door. I didn't notice him until I felt his breath on the back of my neck. I turned to look up at him, and he pressed a finger to his lips.

'Carry on playing,' he said. 'I'll watch.'

I nodded and resumed my game of Super Mario. Aware of him breathing. Aware of him watching me. I couldn't focus on the game and I died.

'Oh, try again,' he said.

'Don't want to,' I replied. 'I'm going to find my mum.'

'Oh, she's in the kitchen with the other aunties. She doesn't want you to spoil her fun.'

I looked at him. He looked back at me, a tiny smile flickering at the corner of his mouth.

'Look how much you've grown,' he said, and reached out to touch my chin. I stood there, frozen. 'Such a big girl you are.'

He moved closer to me and I smelled the whisky on his breath even stronger now. His eyes were cloudy, like he was not focussing on me at all. I'd never seen him like that before. My mum's cousin. Khemu Mama, we called him. I didn't know his proper name.

'Let me see how much you've grown,' he said again and brushed his fingers against my hair. He spread his palms out like the wingspan of a bird. I thought he was going to show me some shadow puppets, so I looked expectantly at the wall opposite. Instead, he touched the front of my choli.

'Remember these are private parts.' Mum's words echoed inside my head. She was telling my sister, while the two of them were sitting in the dining room, drinking tea. 'No one can touch these, except your husband.'

'Eeuw,' my sister spat out her tea. 'Don't be gross, Mum.'

'Touch what?' I'd said, rushing into the room, not wanting to be left out. And my sister had laughed.

'You don't have anything to worry about yet,' she'd said. 'You don't have any boobies yet.'

'Oh, you two,' Mum had said, rolling her eyes. 'But yes, no one touches your boobies, okay? Especially yours.' She'd looked pointedly at my sister and I had felt very separated from the two of them. Like I didn't belong to their little group and their little secrets.

And now he was touching where my boobies would grow. It was wrong, I knew it was wrong. And so, I screamed.

**

I'm retching in the toilet. But nothing comes out. My chest is heaving and I'm crying. For the first time I am crying. I catch the reflection of my breasts in the mirror. They're small. They don't show under the kurta and the dupatta I have on. But I can still feel his hands on my chest. The pressure of his fingers rubbing against the silk blouse. And I vomit. I feel the relief when the pain comes gushing out, filling the toilet bowl with those nightmares.

133

My mother came running through the door and Khemu Mama sprang away from me. He smiled at me like nothing had happened. Then he winked, like this was a secret between us.

'What happened?' Mum said, looking from me to him. 'Why did you scream, Mira?'

I couldn't say anything. He was towering over me.

'Oh, she just got scared. I was trying to show her some shadow puppets—' He spread his hands out again and this time, an eagle soared across the wall, swooping down to sit on the shadow of my head.

'But he touched me here,' I told my mum, pointing to my chest. 'You said nobody could touch me there, except my husband. He's not my husband.'

They stared at each other, and then Mum glared at him. Khemu Mama shrugged and started to leave the room.

'She's lying. I was only trying to entertain her. Stupid girl.'

He walked away and Mum didn't do anything. She kneeled in front of me and I turned away from the stink of whatever she'd been drinking.

'He didn't do anything,' she said finally, dusting off the front of my choli, as if that action erased whatever had just happened. 'Don't worry about it. He won't come back.'

I wanted her to cuddle me, tell me she would keep me safe. But she locked me up in the office, telling me I could play on the Nintendo for as long as I wanted. And that I was never to tell anybody about what had happened. It was all a mistake. And when everybody crowded on the driveway, hugging goodbyes, I saw Khemu Mama give Mum a hug. And she hugged him back, they were laughing, like nothing had happened at all. I lay down on the futon in my dad's study and never played Super Mario ever again.

**

'You alright?'

My sister is knocking on the bathroom door. I summon up all my strength to rise from the floor and stagger towards the door.

'No, I'm not okay. You're not okay. We're both not okay.'

'Mira? What's wrong?'

'No, nothing's wrong now. Everything was wrong from the very beginning. And nobody made it okay for us.'

She hugs me and I feel her body tremble.

'Girls, what's going on? We're waiting to start eating.' Dad's voice booms from the dining room. We look at each other but don't move.

'We're going to tell them the truth, yes?' She shakes her head in terror, but I grip her hand so tight that she cries out.

'You're not going to leave home to settle down here just because our parents cannot deal with 'the shame' of you not living up to their expectations. They have to face the truth.'

'I know,' she says. 'But will they? They have a reputation to protect. And I can't be the reason that they—'

'But you're not the reason. They have done this to themselves. They have done this to us. To you. To me.'

'You?' She cannot comprehend what I've just said. And then, 'You too?'

I nod, and her face crumples. 'Not you too.'

We hold each other close. The truth is far too painful for either of us at this moment.

'Come,' I finally say to her. 'This is the perfect time. They are all sitting there, eating together.'

'Are You sure?'

I nod and reach out for her hand. 'Will you come with me? Will you speak in your defence?'

**

'Here's what we will do,' I say to her.

'You will tell them point blank what has happened.

You will tell them that you refuse to compromise on your future.

You will tell them that your sexual assault is not your burden alone.

You will tell them to own it and deal with it with you.

You will tell them that you will live your life the way you want.

And I will tell them what I've been made to hide for ten years.

I will tell Mum that I cannot keep it a secret anymore.

I will tell her to deal with the truth.

I will tell them that they will have to support us, no matter what.'

**

I wait for her to react, and slowly she says yes. She holds my hand and we walk towards the dining room. Everyone is looking at us expectantly. I nod to her and the two of us swoop in. Dinner will have to wait.

Bird

Jupiter Jones

Bowen had been disturbed in the night by the owls. Their haunting *Hoooo-hooo* was a familiar lullaby but their other noise always woke him.

Keee-ick, keeeeee-ick.

This side of the forestry, one of them had caught something and it was bragging, calling out: *Gotcha*! The owl would be holding the catch in its claws, bending over it, ripping off bits of fur and flesh, not savouring morsels, but indiscriminately swallowing sinew, intestines, bone, everything. It was too late in the year now to be feeding owlets; this was a banquet for one. Bowen slept fitfully and dreamt of his estranged wife.

When morning eventually came, it was a dreary one. He watched the light beyond his uncurtained window gradually increase from green to grey and judged it to be approaching six-thirty, but by the time he had his trousers on, it was almost seven and the dog was waiting by his boots at the bottom of the stairs.

'Hey Fly, Wotcha!' he said, and the tri-coloured collie acknowledged his greeting with a slight twitch of her brow. He unbolted the back door and they stepped out into the dank but mild morning to sniff the air, and side-by-side, they peed companionably behind the tangled hedgerow. Fly squatted but there was a twitch of her left hind leg as if she

137

almost thought she might cock it to make a tripod of herself. As Bowen fastened his trousers, he suppressed a smile.

He could hear Maude was beginning to fret, plucking at her cage; maybe the owls had woken her in the night too. She would have to wait; she'd been with him for fifteen years now, much longer than Fly, and she was used to his ways. Today was not a good day, and he limped as he pottered about the kitchen, frying streaky bacon and bread for himself and getting kibble for Fly, and limped as he washed up, wiped and put away, and as he swept the floor. He rolled a cigarette and stood in the doorway with all his weight on his good leg and looked up the valley.

There were no houses up there; his was the last habitation before the dam and the reservoir of dark water. It had taken years to build, finished back in 1928, with who knows how many lives lost in the construction. They pumped the water down south, to some sprawling thirsty town, miles away. Not that he begrudged that, begrudged them the water. This valley got more than its fair share and could easily spare some. Only now, the water was condemned as undrinkable, discoloured and tainted by the peat that washed into it, and those lost lives seemed especially wasteful.

In the distance, he could see a curl of grey smoke rising into the windless sky.

'No fire without smoke,' he said to Fly, and she blinked back at him.

It was late November; leaves blanketed the wet ground and the bare trees rested. The fire was unlikely to be a problem – most likely some clown, wild camping, a stunt to prove they could hack it outdoors in the cold, some survival goon with a bivouac. In the summer there was a steady influx of brown trout fishermen and garish mountain-bikers, but this late in the year Bowen rarely saw anyone, and Maude certainly expected to have the place to herself; she was the self-appointed queen of the valley. Usually, if Bowen was going up to the old reservoir, he would make his way up through the field, perhaps stuffing his pockets with the last of the mushrooms, up through his patch of woodland, checking on last year's coppicing, then on through the green cathedral of the Forestry Commission hushed by its decades-thick carpet of pine needles. But today, with his stump giving him gyp, he walked up the road: single track, few passing places.

**

As soon as he comes into focus in his sludge-coloured coat, and green woolly hat grafted onto his head, even before I can begin to make out the thundery expression on the old geezer's face, I guess there'll be ructions. He makes slow progress up the road, leaning into the gradient, and I brace myself for a get-off-of-my-land kind of a row. He's got a dog, slinking along beside him, giving me the evil eye.

'Are you lost, lad?' the man shouts.

I stand and give him the thumbs up by way of greeting. Shit, why'd I do that? What a dope, what a nerdy gesture. He keeps on coming and I see a look of uncertainty or puzzlement pass over his face, then it hardens to the disgust and resentment that I'm getting used to. Why should I expect it to be any different up here?

'Is it far? To the old reservoir?' I call out, though I already know it's just over a mile. I drove up there yesterday as the light was fading, then I turned the campervan around in front of the hideous dark wall that blocks the valley and trundled back looking for a less intimidating overnight campsite – though in truth, it is all dismal round here, and not at all how I imagined it would be.

The old man pulls off his beanie hat and scratches the flat hair beneath as he looks me quite literally up and down; as he takes in my dress, my reddish stubble, watery-blue eyes, strong jaw, dress, rigger boots, dress. *Floral* dress.

'What the fuckin-fish are you, then?' he says.

The tin kettle balanced on the primus stove begins its breathy whistle as we stand there, scowling, facing each other like gunfighters in a Spaghetti Western. We square up, arms hanging out from our sides, fists curled loosely, palms itching, and all that's missing from the scene is tumbleweed. The old man's bullish gaze skewers me, but I glare back with all the defiance I can muster. If I were a fighting man, I should fancy my chances; he's old, sixty maybe, and shorter than me, but stocky. I'd have better reach and speed, but I've always been a wuss and I can't throw a decent punch. The kettle shrieks like a banshee.

'A tranny?' he says. 'A flaming tranny?'

'Would you like a cup of tea?'

The old man looks like he might actually explode with affront, then he starts to shake his head as if in disbelief, then chuckle, then proper belly laughs.

'Is it not a bit cold, a bit draughty, out here, in a frock?'

I flip up the hem of my dress, not coquettishly, but to show the navy fleece joggers beneath, and he grunts and takes a pew on the log I've dragged up to my campfire.

'That's a piss-poor fire you have there, lad – lass, whatever, I don't rightly know if you're a bloke or a bird.'

'Michael.'

'Bowen.' He nods to me and then stretches out his legs and he winces a bit. 'Your wood's sopping wet.'

And of course he is right, the damp twigs and pinecones I had gathered are smouldering, and the bigger bits of branches, though charred, have refused to catch – but at least

I have the primus. So I fetch a second tin mug from the van and make the tea, and the man takes off his boot and a prosthetic foot. He rubs the stump of his leg below the knee.

'You should have gone deeper into the forest for some drier stuff.'

'No sugar, I'm afraid,' I say, and he shrugs. The dog settles with its nose between its paws and its ginger eyebrows twitching.

As we sip our tea, he says nothing, just watches me and the silence starts off sort-of edgy and calcifies into awkward, and feeling under pressure, I start to jabber. I tell him about Aunty Dilys, how she was my grandfather's aunt really, but everyone called her Aunty Dilys, even people who weren't related to her in the slightest, they all knew her as Aunty Dilys.

'She was born here, well, somewhere in this valley and was orphaned when she was just a few weeks old. Her mother got that purp – puerperal fever and her father was killed in the blasting. She got brought up by three older brothers, so she said.'

I show him the jam jar of grey-gritty remains from the crematorium.

'I've brought her home,' I say.

'Jeez, was she a midget? There's not much of her.'

I shake the jar like it's a snow globe and the dust and granulated bone fragments of her cloud the glass and settle in a clump at the bottom. 'The family couldn't agree on where she was to be laid to rest, or sprinkled, or flung into the wind, so we divvied her up. This is my portion.'

The man, Bowen, rubs the blunt end of his leg some more; he looks thoughtful, and I wonder if he's thinking about which part of her is in the jar. Is it a foot? A liver, a shin? It's what I've been wondering. And then I'm needled by another

141

awkward thought, I want to ask him about what had happened to him, how come he'd had a piece of himself amputated, and what happened to the part they cut off. Is it saved somewhere to be reunited with the rest of him when he croaks? No, that's ridiculous, we can't save every part, or we'd be storing up nail clippings. Still, a foot is different, more significant. I feel heat beginning on my chest, and I just know the colour is rising up my throat, rising up my face, mottling my cheeks. Why'd I have such damn-fool inappropriate thoughts? I'm always doing it, making such a tit of myself. And once I think about the stupidity of the thought, then I'm mortified. I should have grown out of this by now. Uncomfortably, I twist the soft fabric of my dress, swallow hard, my skin blazing hot. The dress slips through my fingers and disappears, leaving me naked; the old man can see through my skin and bone, see into my skull and know my thoughts.

'Actually she was quite tall,' I say, hurrying to stop thinking what he must surely know I'm thinking. 'Astonishingly tall for a woman, nearly six foot in her prime, which is a lot for a woman even now, but back then, she must have been quite the freak, and she never married or had any children. She scared me a bit when I was a child, the way she didn't ever take her eyes off me, but she always tried to be kind, I think, I'm sure she meant to be kind, and she bought me a book about otters, though she never learned to read herself, *book-learning* she called it. I suppose she must have been lonely, living on her own all those years and having trouble finding shoes to fit.'

Bowen looks at me, head cocked. He keeps looking but doesn't interrupt me or offer any comment, so I rattle on.

'She was ninety-three when she died, and she never went into a home or anything; she lived without central heating or

142

any mod-cons really; and she was a hard worker, always, and until she retired, she worked on the railways. This is one of her dresses.'

It all comes out in a blurt. Words tumbling over themselves, and I feel such an idiot. Why'd I tell him all that? It's not like he asked. I'm panting a bit, out of breath, my lungs snatch at the air, my chest is tight, the back of my eyes pricking with hot stinging tears. Get a grip, fool. Don't cry. Boys don't. Never taking my brimming eyes off Bowen's face, I wipe my nose with the heel of my hand.

**

Bowen could see that the boy was in a bate. When the words stopped coming, Bowen looked away and rested his eyes on the murky depths of the forestry picking out the fluorescent daubs on the trunks earmarked for felling. He drank the tea in silence, then swirled the last bit around the tin mug and tossed it onto the grass; the liquid briefly arced and glittered in the morning light. The boy was quiet again, spent and subdued, staring into the eye-watering smoke. Bowen fastened his prosthetic foot back on, adjusted the laces of his boot, then stood up, testing his weight on it, testing the familiar pain. He walked over, put his hand on Michael's shoulder, leaning on him a moment, breathing in a familiar scent of Yardley lavender soap.

'You done her proud, Michael. Bringing her home.'

He whistled to his dog, and they headed back down the valley, between the silent green-black pines, through the naked woodlands, over the ill-kept tussocky fields. By his side, Fly bounded about, her wet black nose frequently exploring the turf or the bracken, then she'd belt after him to catch up. And on his other side, the Gwryne Fawr, not yet

143

fully a river was always hustling ahead of him, tumbling and gushing over a multitude of rocks. Down the valley they went, heading home, back to Maude. He would let her out, he would fly her a while, watch her soar and swoop over her kingdom, likely she'd get a couple of rabbits to stew for dinner. He will skin and joint them; Maude shall have the hearts and livers.

Dogs in a Storm

Brennig Davies

Mary-Ann awakes with a *fuck it* feeling. *I really must get that seen to,* she thinks, snoozing the alarm (hungry for sleep). *Let the kids find their own way to school. They're old enough now.*

On the news, the weatherman says that a storm is coming, and she begins to understand. Her mother always said that dogs go mad when the thunder starts, barking and frantic. Maybe this is why her skin itches; why all her blood is playing jazz. Maybe she's one more dog in a storm — lit up by the electricity, passing cloud to cloud.

She tries to calm herself. She makes the boys packed lunches: a Dairylea triangle and an apple each. Thomas asks about sandwiches, and she just tells him to get in the car. She speeds the whole way to school. On her way home she stops by the shops, and sweeps the shelves of things she knows she doesn't need: hair dye (which she has never used before); a pack of plastic sporks (when has she ever used a spork?); a large scratching post for the cat (they do not have, and have never had, a cat). Back in the house, the unpacking confuses her, because none of it belongs anywhere. She wonders if she is losing her mind — there is something almost obscenely funny in the idea, and it makes her cackle.

She tries to do a handstand against the kitchen wall and fails (which makes sense, having never attempted one before). On the way down, she bangs her ankle on the work surface, and yelps in pain; collapsed on the floor, the yelping turns to laughter again. *It is 10am,* she thinks, *and I feel pissed as a fart.* She laughs harder. *Pissed as a fart. What does that even mean? What has it ever meant?* She never normally swears, but in her head she has been swearing all morning, like a sailor. Like a *bloody fucking sodding* sailor.

She hears a rumbling in the distance.

The home phone rings, suddenly, and she answers. 'Yello?' she says, like people in films. She thinks, *I am genuinely so funny, I might make myself piss myself (piss myself like a fart).*

'Mary-Ann?'

It is her mother on the end of the line. *Oh, Christ.* She imagines her at home, sitting tight-lipped, straight-backed, like a malevolent toilet attendant.

'Mary-Ann, is that you?' her mother repeats.

'No,' says Mary-Ann. 'It's her twin sister.' She thinks for a second, then adds: 'Marianne.' (When she was younger, she'd asked her mother to call her Marianne instead. 'Why on earth would I do that?' her mother had said, staring at her, killing the conversation dead. *What I should have said,* Mary-Ann thinks, *is because Mary-Ann is dowdy, but Marianne is chic. Marianne would live in London or Paris, editing magazines, wearing pantsuits so sharp they could cut; Mary-Ann lives in a cul-de-sac, owner of fifty sporks she knows she won't use.* It wouldn't have mattered. Her mother would just have paused, pursed her lips, and spat: *only lesbians wear trousers, Mary-Ann.*)

'Mary-Ann,' her mother says now, 'what's the matter? Have you been drinking?'

'I'm fine, Mother,' she replies. 'Just pissed as a fart!' She thinks, *have I always been this funny, or has it just come over me all of a sudden? I should consider doing stand-up. People ought to hear me.*

'Mary-Ann, don't be vulgar. It doesn't suit you. Where is Declan? Is he there?'

'He's at work.' (Her husband has an office job she doesn't fully understand, and she's not wholly convinced he does either. But he's there, nine to five, five days a week, and seems to enjoy the ritual of it. He enjoys waking up and putting on a shirt and tie, kissing the boys on their heads and Mary-Ann on the cheek as he leaves, briefcase in hand. *Why does he carry a briefcase? That's a bit weird, isn't it? Who the fuck has a briefcase anymore?*)

'Oh,' her mother says, 'of course. Well, what are you doing with yourself today?'

'Just this and that.'

She thinks, *I used to do things, lots of things. I used to read! I used to read loads of books, and discuss those books with people. And I enjoyed it, I was good at it; I got a First. And now I just drive to a random house, once a month, to talk about* Life of Pi *with a bunch of women who have not read it, and whom I do not even like.* She has a sudden urge to hang up the phone and run a marathon, run and run and not look back.

Outside, it starts to rain.

Her mother says, 'You could start by cleaning that house of yours. Like a pigsty, the last time I came.'

'Maybe I just like wallowing in my own filth.'

'Mary-Ann, what is *wrong* with you today? You're being very disagreeable. I didn't raise you to be disagreeable.'

'Nothing's wrong, Mother. I'm just very busy, that's all. Was there something you wanted, before I go?'

'Well, I just wanted to see how you were.'

'I'm great! Anything else?'

Her mother pauses, stalling for time. 'My hip has been playing up again. I knew I should have gone private. And Jean has a new guide-dog: disgusting thing, slobbers everywhere. But of course *Jean* can't see that, so what does she care? Oh, and Sally Gough has come back to live with her

147

mother, since the fall. I saw her going into the house yesterday with the shopping. She always was such a caring girl.'

Maura Gough has lived on the same street as Mary-Ann's mother for years. Mary-Ann and Sally had gone to university together; at one point they'd been close, and then had drifted apart over time (*sad, how people do that,* she thinks). The last she'd heard, Sally had been working for an NGO, delivering clean water to the third world (her mother's words). And now she's back.

I should reach out to her, Mary-Ann thinks, *on Facebook or something.* She remembers one time in their second year, when she had sat with Sally on the pavement outside a nightclub, discussing *To the Lighthouse,* of all things, and Sally had brushed a strand of hair behind her ear in that way she always did and Mary-Ann had felt such a wrench, such a violent *lurch* of emotion towards her, that she wanted to lean in towards her and kiss her on the mouth. Sometimes, even now, she wishes she had, for she had felt, in that moment, a little like a dog in a storm: giddy and excited and restless. Like something deep inside her was leap leaping up; some creature, craving something she did not know it could crave.

She looks around the kitchen, at all the surfaces and shelves and mugs in the corner. *How did I become the kind of person with a cupboard full of frying pans, when at one time, I was a dog in a storm?* She stares at the magnets on the fridge, the microwave, the hair dye and the scratching post and the sporks. Meaningless, all of it, to the point of being absurd, but an absurd that falls just short of funny, all of a sudden.

Her mother is still speaking, but Mary-Ann hangs up while she's mid-sentence. The phone rings again, and again, and outside it starts raining even harder.

**

Mary-Ann sits on the bathroom floor, applying the hair dye. *Sunset Red.* It looks absolutely ridiculous, and she absolutely loves it. She'd considered cracking open a bottle of Prosecco, to glug over the sink while the stuff sank into her scalp, but decided against it. She feels drunk enough without it.

And she genuinely does feel drunk. It must be the rain that's been battering down outside the window all afternoon; the slow drizzle, which gave way to lashings and spatterings and gallons, full gallons of water being spat from the sky.

She sees it fall and thinks, *Good. Good, let's have a bloody flood. Let's have a big Noah flood and flush away all the shit. All the shit we have to pretend to like and think and feel and leave only the other stuff.* She doesn't question exactly what she thinks will be left, but she knows she wants to be someone else. She wants the storm to come, to flay her skin from her bones. To swallow her up, gobble her. She wants the storm to pick her up in its big, strong, King Kong grasp, and fling her around; she wants to fall to the ground and be Marianne in Paris, in a pantsuit.

When the kids get home from school, they ask if she's okay, and she says, 'I'm fine, I'm fine, how are you?'

Her youngest says, 'I saw lightning through the window during Maths last lesson,' and normally she'd feel obligated to say *Why weren't you concentrating on Maths?* But today she says, 'Describe it for me.'

He looks at her, his small eyebrow raised. *This child came out of me,* she thinks, *and I don't even know him. He certainly doesn't know me.* 'What do you mean?' he says.

She says, 'Describe the lightning.'

At first he seems wary. And then he says, 'It was big, and bright and…jagged,' and she says, 'Good, good, that's good,' and again he says, 'Mum, are you sure you're okay?'

'Joe, I'm fine. Would people please stop asking me if I'm okay?'

149

His face falls, but she is tired of consoling. He asks, 'What happened to your hair?'

'It's called *Sunset Red*, actually — do you like it?'

'I'm not sure.'

'Well, I do,' she snaps. 'I like it a lot.'

'When's dinner?' he asks, and she says, 'Go eat some Dairylea if you're hungry,' and he says, 'Mum, why are you so obsessed with Dairylea all of a sudden?'

She bursts into tears. A slow drizzle gives way to lashings and spatterings and gallons.

**

She hears Declan's car in the driveway, then his feet on the stairs. 'Mary-Ann, sweetheart,' he says, stepping carefully into the room, sitting down beside her, his briefcase still in hand. 'The children are getting a bit scared now.'

She doesn't stop crying. *He is a good man; a gentle, kind man. So why do I want to howl and howl and never stop? I could throw my head back right now and bay like a hound. It's not just the storm, it isn't, it isn't.*

'Your mother rang me,' Declan says. 'She said you sounded strange on the phone earlier. I think she's worried about you.'

She says nothing. Outside, the rain beats Biblical. She looks at Declan, at his suit and white socks, and thinks, *Never once have you made me orgasm. Not properly. All that missionary (always, always missionary), and…nothing, really.* She thinks, *All I've ever really wanted is an excuse to shriek and you have never, ever given me it.*

But now the storm is here, so maybe this is my chance. And if I start now, god knows I might never stop.

She closes her eyes and imagines the rain shattering the

pavements outside. *Maybe there will be deep fissures, chasms in the earth. Maybe we'll all fall in.*

'I need to go for a walk,' she says, suddenly.

He looks at her. 'Mary-Ann, you can't go out in this. It's chucking it down.'

For some reason, just this phrase, the way he says it, makes her want to cry even harder. *Chucking it down.* People say it all the time; he says it all the time. *But how can it all be so predictable, and still so utterly beyond my control?* She wishes he had said something else. *He should have said: it's raining cats and dogs.*

'I'm taking the dog for a walk,' she says, and he says, 'But we don't have a dog.'

She steps out into the downpour regardless.

**

It's the glove, Sally had said, on the pavement outside that nightclub all those years ago. Mary-Ann can't even remember the name of the nightclub, but she remembers this. *In* To the Lighthouse, Sally had said; *it's the bit with the glove that I love best.*

She was pissed as a fart, but still speaking more sense than anyone else Mary-Ann had met on the course. She always spoke with such conviction.

At one point, Sally continued, *Virginia Woolf says that Mrs Ramsey's presence is so strong, that if you found a crumpled-up glove on the sofa, you'd know it was hers, just by the way the finger was twisted. Isn't that amazing? To just...BE so strongly, that you just kind of echo through everything you've ever touched. Know what I mean?*

Yeah, Mary-Ann had said, staring at her, longing to be touched. *I know exactly what you mean.*

151

Mary-Ann walks through the sheets of rain, past the branches of lightning blooming all around her in the sky: the static, clinging, the winds, picking up.

All her blood jives.

She walks to the park across the road from the house and sits on a swing, thinking about the glove. She looks down at her hands, and gently starts to peel away the skin: it comes off in long, neat strips, like wallpaper. She keeps going until she can see exposed flesh, the shades of muscle and sinew and veins running spider right through her, and she can feel the cold, cold rain falling directly onto her nerves.

Mrs Owen from No. 42 owns two grey whippets, beautiful creatures, sleek and fragile and strong. *They must have escaped through the back door,* Mary-Ann thinks, as she sees them cross the park towards her. *I guess even dogs in a storm roam in packs.*

When the whippets reach her, they help her slough off the rest of her skin with their claws and pointy little teeth.

She gets up from the swing; the dogs stand up on their hind legs. All three stand in a circle; she holds a paw in each of her naked hands. Then, slowly, in the circle, they all begin to skip, *round and round and round, dancing to the sound of the swirl of the world*, and Mary-Ann throws back her head, and bellows. The other dogs, too, start to bay at the moon like wolves.

It's the glove, Sally had said, and Mary-Ann had wanted so desperately to kiss her, to make love to her, to feel them echo through each other.

I could have been Marianne with Sally.

I might have been Marianne.

The wind rises and rises, until Mary-Ann is lifted off her feet with the whippets, into the air, spinning as lightning flashes all around but never strikes, a tune playing somewhere far away: *dogs go mad in a storm,*

Don't be vulgar, it doesn't suit you,

big and bright and jagged,

it's called Sunset Red,

chucking it down,

chuck it down,

the glove, the glove, the glove...

Imagine being so strongly, Sally had said. *I don't want to wake up one morning and find I haven't been in the world. You know? It's one thing not to live properly, but it's another not to be.*

The animal in Mary-Ann's chest had scratched and whined and she had left it locked up. Now she squeezes the paws of the whippets, and feels her own tender flesh pulse and bleed, cringing by instinct.

Well, fuck it, she thinks. *Drink life down to the lees.*

And suddenly the rain stops, and she is back on the ground, alone in the park. The dogs have vanished. Everything is very quiet, again; it is almost as if nothing has happened.

She picks up her mobile from the mound of her crumpled clothes and skin on the grass. Eleven missed calls from Declan, and fourteen texts.

Sweetheart, are you alright?

Mary-Ann, the children are worried.

Please ring me if you get this.

Mary-Ann, if you don't ring me back soon, I'm calling the police.

He'll probably have called them by now, she thinks. *There'll be blue lights soon.* She starts pulling her skin back onto her body when she stops and thinks of *To the Lighthouse,* of quoting, in a seminar, how

...nothing so solaced her, eased her of the perplexity of life, and

miraculously raised its burdens, as this sublime power, this heavenly gift, and one would no more disturb it, while it lasted, than break up the shaft of sunlight, lying level across the floor...

With half her skin still stripped off, she sends a Facebook friend request to Sally Gough.

It is accepted immediately. The animal in her chest leaps up.

Hi, Sally, she types on Messenger. *Not sure if you remember me, but I just wanted to reach out to you.*

She waits, but not for long. Three bubbles ripple on the screen, and then:

Of course I remember you, Sally writes. *Hello, Marianne.*

Author Biographies

Susmita Bhattacharya's debut novel, *The Normal State of Mind* (Parthian, 2015) was longlisted for the Word2Screen Prize at the Mumbai Film Festival, 2018. Her short story collection, *Table Manners* (Dahlia Publishing, 2018) won the Saboteur Award for Best Short Story Collection (2019) and has been featured on BBC Radio 4. She has an MA in Creative Writing from Cardiff University and is a lecturer at Winchester University. She also facilitates the ArtfulScribe Mayflower Young Writers programme in Southampton. Susmita lives in Winchester. Twitter: @Susmitatweets

Brennig Davies is a writer from the Vale of Glamorgan, south Wales. He recently completed his BA in English at Mansfield College, Oxford, and in the past his work has won the inaugural BBC Young Writers Award in 2015 and the Crown at the Urdd National Eisteddfod 2019. He has also been published in the *Oxford Review of Books*, the *Mays Anthology XXIX*, and Kate Clanchy's anthology *Friend: poems by young people* (Picador, 2021).

Giancarlo Gemin was born in Cardiff in 1962 of Italian parentage. He has written two children's books, *Cowgirl*, which won the Tir na n-Og award in 2015 and was shortlisted for the Waterstones Prize, and *Sweet Pizza*, which was longlisted for the Guardian Children's Fiction Prize 2016 and won the Tir na n-Og award in 2017. He is working on his first adult novel about a library in Wales during the austerity years.

Craig Hawes is a journalist-turned-copywriter from Briton Ferry who worked in London and Dubai for many years before returning to south Wales. His short story collection, *The Witch Doctor of Umm Suqeim*, was published in 2013 by Parthian Books and his plays and stories have been broadcast on BBC Radio 4. He was shortlisted for the Rhys Davies Short Story Prize in 2010. Twitter: @CRHawes1

Chloë Heuch was born in Taunton and lives near Pwllheli on the north Wales coast with her family. She has a Creative Writing MA from Lancaster University and is a member of SCBWI and SoA. She has had poems and short stories published in the past, the latter through Honno press. Her debut YA novel, *Too Dark to See*, was published in 2020 through Firefly Press. Find out more at www.chloëheuch.co.uk. Twitter: @clogsulike

Philippa Holloway is a writer and senior lecturer at Staffordshire University, living in England but with her heart still at home in Wales. Her short fiction is published on four continents and her debut novel, *The Half-life of Snails*, is due out with Parthian Books in spring 2022. She is co-editor of the collection *100 Words of Solitude: Global Voices in Lockdown 2020* (Rare Swan Press). Twitter: @thejackdawspen

Joshua Jones is a queer, autistic writer and poet from Llanelli, south Wales. He has an MA in Creative Writing from Bath Spa University, where he worked on his debut collection of short stories, and is currently studying to become a teacher at Cardiff Met. He also likes to paint and make collages, and releases poetry with music under the name Human Head. He writes about music for *Nawr Magazine*, and his personal blog/portfolio can be found at www.ermose.com. Twitter: @nothumanhead Insta: @joshuajonespoet

Jupiter Jones grew up on the north-west coasts of Cumberland and Lancashire. The first was wild and secretive, the second trashy and jaded; she loved them both and they haunt her writing. Following a brief spell in London to complete a PhD in Spectatorial Embarrassment at Goldsmiths, she now lives in Wales and writes short and flash fictions. She is the winner of the Colm Tóibín International Prize, and her work has been published by Ad Hoc Fiction, Aesthetica, Brittle Star, Fish Publishing, Reflex Press, Scottish Arts Trust, and rejected by many, many others.

Kate Lockwood Jefford was born and grew up in Cardiff. She trained as a psychiatrist and psychotherapist and worked in the NHS – alongside a stint writing and performing stand-up comedy – before completing an MA in Creative Writing at Birkbeck. Her short fiction appears in many publications including *Mechanics' Institute Review* (MIR) online, *Bristol Prize Anthology 2017*, *Brick Lane Bookshop 2020 Prize Anthology* and *Fish Publishing Prize Anthology 2021*. Her short story, 'Picasso's Face', won the 2020 VS Pritchett Prize. Currently living in London & Folkestone, she still spends a lot of time in south Wales, either in person or in her mind. She is working on her first collection of stories. Twitter: @kljefford

Rosie Manning grew up in Pembrokeshire and spent her childhood obsessed with books and seeing the rest of the world. She left at eighteen and spent ten years travelling, studying, working, and travelling some more until the west coast pulled her home. A graduate in English Literature & Philosophy from the University of Sussex, she recently completed an MA in Creative Writing, with Distinction, at the Open University. Rosie now works in her local library while writing her first novel and a short story collection. 'Juice' is her first publication. Twitter: @RosieMayfly

Naomi Paulus was born, and had most of her formative experiences, in Swansea. She graduated with a degree in Philosophy from the University of Cambridge, after which she spent a year at the Cambridge Judge Business School learning some practical skills. At thirty she decided to start writing down thoughts as well as just thinking them. She has been longlisted for the Primadonna Prize twice and won their 2020 flash fiction competition. She runs a digital agency in London in her spare time. Twitter: @napapolis

Elizabeth Pratt is a transplanted American who took root in the UK way back in the carefree 90's. She lives happily in west Wales with her fella, a few cats, and an untamed vegetable garden. She's enamoured with writing short stories and flash fiction of all genres but has also been hard at work on her first novel. She won the HE Bates Short Story Competition in 2018 and the Frome Festival Short Story Competition in 2020. She also writes as Elizabeth Ardith Aylward.

PARTHIAN Fiction

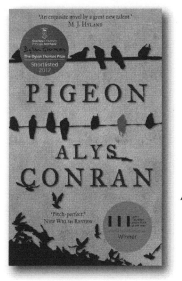

Pigeon

ALYS CONRAN
ISBN 978-1-910901-23-6
£8.99 • Paperback

**Winner of Wales
Book of the Year**

'**An exquisite novel by a great
new talent.'** – M.J. Hyland

Ironopolis

GLEN JAMES BROWN
ISBN 978-1-912681-09-9
£10.99 • Paperback

**Shortlisted for the Orwell
Award for Political Fiction and
the Portico Prize**

'**A triumph'** – *The Guardian*

'**The most accomplished
working-class novel of the
last few years.'** – *Morning Star*

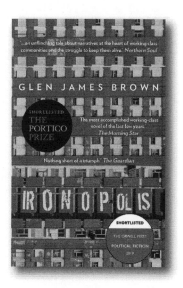

PARTHIAN Fiction

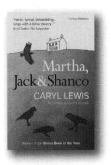

Martha, Jack & Shanco

CARYL LEWIS

TRANSLATED BY GWEN DAVIES

ISBN 978-1-912681-77-8

£9.99 • Paperback

Winner of the Wales Book of the Year

'Harsh, lyrical, devastating... sings with a bitter poetry.' – *The Independent*

Love and Other Possibilities

LEWIS DAVIES

ISBN 978-1-906998-08-0

£6.99 • Paperback

Winner of the Rhys Davies Award

'Davies's prose is simple and effortless, the kind of writing that wins competitions.' – *The Independent*

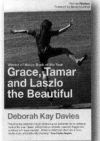

Grace, Tamar and Laszlo the Beautiful

DEBORAH KAY DAVIES

ISBN 978-1-912109-43-2

£8.99 • Paperback

Winner of the Wales Book of the Year

'Davies's writing thrills on all levels.' – Suzy Ceulan Hughes

Hummingbird

TRISTAN HUGHES

ISBN 978-1-91090-90-8

£10 • Hardback

£8.99 • Paperback

Winner of the Stanford Fiction Award

'Superbly accomplished... Hughes's prose is startling and luminous.' – *Financial Times*

PARTHIAN   Fiction

The Web of Belonging

STEVIE DAVIES
ISBN 978-1-912681-16-7
£8.99 • Paperback

'A comic novelist of
the highest order.'
– *The Times*

The Cormorant

STEPHEN GREGORY
ISBN 978-1-912681-69-3
£8.99 • Paperback

Winner of the
Somerset Maugham Award
'A first-class terror story with a
relentless focus that would have made
Edgar Allan Poe proud.'
– *The New York Times*

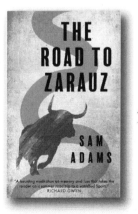

The Road to Zarauz

SAM ADAMS
ISBN 978-1-912681-85-3
£8.99 • Paperback
'A haunting meditation on memory and
loss that takes the reader on a summer
road trip to a vanished Spain.'
– Richard Gwyn

PARTHIAN   Fiction

Angels of Cairo

GARY RAYMOND

ISBN 978-1-913640-28-6

£9 • Paperback

'A book full of wisdom
and wit and warmth...'
– Stephen Gregory

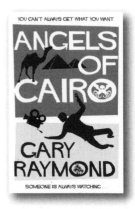

Easy Meat

RACHEL TREZISE

ISBN 978-1-912681-24-2

£9 • Paperback

'*Easy Meat* feels like a monumental
achievement. A one-sitting page-turner
that gives voice to the voiceless.'
– *The National*

The Scrapbook

CARLY HOLMES

ISBN 978-1-910409-83-1

£8.99 • Paperback

'An impressive debut novel from an
extremely talented writer.'
– *Wales Arts Review*

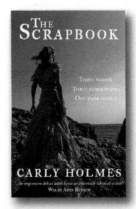